Revenant

The Fortress Book 2

T. A. Styles

TRANSCENDANCE PRESS

Revenant

ISBN: 979-8-9879684-2-0 (Trade Paperback)

ISBN: 979-8-9879684-3-7 (eBook)

Contents

One

Happy birthday to you. Happy birthday to you. Happy birthday, dear Baby. Happy birthday to you.

"Are you one," Teddy howled. "Are you two, are you three, are you four, are you five…"

Soon after, Wyatt, Misty, Leo, Sky, King, Miracle, JZ, and Yamil joined the chanting bedlam.

Are you six, are you seven, are you eight, are you nine, are you ten—

"Stop!" Baby cried, holding out an arm.

Then came a silence across the dining room as Baby hovered over a small chocolate cake slathered with peanut butter, crowned with ten lighted candles. She leaned in, pulling aside her blonde locks, which had grown much longer since Sim's death, and blew out the ten little flames with one giant huff. Everyone clapped as she straightened up and smiled.

"Is it really my birthday?" Baby asked. "And am I really ten?"

"Who knows," Leo shrugged while adjusting his glasses on the bridge of his nose. "You know how Sim figured it."

Sim calculated the birthdays of his orphans using the annual hashmarks from when they arrived at the fortress, along with what their presumed ages had been at the time of that arrival. He had found Baby milling about in the trash and had no idea how old she was, so in her case, he had to assume. She did remember, not her birthday, but that she had been in the first grade.

Six or seven, then.

And then the fact that she had arrived at the fortress three years ago. So, she was ten.

"And what about this cake?" Baby said. "We've never eaten a fortress cake before. Is it going to make us sick?"

Teddy shrugged. "Probably."

Sky started pulling the candles from the cake. "It was made with flour that Sim kept in mylar bags with oxygenators, so at least that ingredient should be fine, as well as the peanut butter topping. As far as the sugar, baking powder, and cocoa, it's anyone's guess."

"Don't forget about how it was baked," King mocked.

"Gosh dang it," Wyatt said. "Stop making fun of my solar oven. Solar energy is the key to our future of unlocking more feasible electric power. Look at that cake; it's a thing of beauty."

Wyatt had been assigned by Charlie to stay at the fortress after Sim's death so that there was an adult presence in the home. Sky and King weren't especially elated that they were not recognized by the committee of five, including Charlie, Wyatt, Misty, King, and Sky, to oversee the fortress operations. But in the end, they couldn't complain, because it was Misty who split the vote in favor of having Wyatt assigned there.

We are still only children, after all. Sim knew this, and so this is what he would want.

Sky understood Misty's logic and that having an acknowledged adult at the fortress would ease the anxiety of some of the orphans, but she was ambivalent about Wyatt being the adult selected for the job.

He's not the brightest bulb in the box.

She did not put up much fuss, however, as it was her and King predominantly making the decisions for the fortress. Wyatt was a puppet, as they perceived him.

"It may look like a thing of beauty," Leo said, "but we'll see if it tastes like a thing of beauty."

"Cake," Misty said. "It can taste terrible, but it's still...cake. One time, when I was young, my mother made the most beautiful cake for my birthday. It was white with pink sprinkles. I think I was six, and even though I invited ten of my classmates, only two showed. It was still fun, but there was so much cake left over. I would wake up late at night and come down and raid the refrigerator, and every morning my mother would look at the cake and think it was my father who ate it. She yelled at him because he had the diabetes. He would tell her it wasn't him that ate it, but she never believed him."

"Enough talk," Baby said, whipping out from her waistline one of her Ka-bar knives and slicing into the cake. It was moist—perhaps too much so. When Baby pulled up the knife, half the cake came with it.

"OMG," JZ shouted. "Don't expect me to be eatin' any of that gross stuff."

"I'm sure it tastes fine," Sky said. "It's the first cake we've had in nearly four years. We have to celebrate!"

"Not before she makes a wish," Leo said.

"I almost forgot," Sky said. She pulled the coin from her pocket. "When I flip it into the air, make a wish and call it."

Baby closed her eyes as Sky flipped Kellogg's coin. She caught it in her right hand and quickly smacked it onto the back of her left, keeping it concealed.

"Heads," Baby called.

Sky uncovered the coin, and it was heads up. "It looks like your wish will come true."

Baby smiled, but as they were about to serve the cake, Gigi kicked into a ferocious bark. She was standing on her hind legs, barking madly with her front paws perched on the windowsill. The others grabbed their weapons and ran to the windows, which had been unbricked since the days of Zagan. The shutters were open, so the view of the street was clear.

They crowded around and peered out, the little ones finding gaps between their older counterparts so they could see. There were five men standing together across the street in a cluster. They were staring blankly at the fortress until one of the men, an older man, waved.

Yamil waved back and Sky pushed his hand down. "What are you doing, Yamil?"

"What do *they* want?" King asked. "They don't look like wanderers."

"Whose turn is it to vet?" Sky asked.

"Wyatt never vets anyone," King said.

"I've vetted plenty of people at the heights," Wyatt hissed. "But if you're saying you want me to go out there and see what's what, that's what I'll do."

"Okay, then," King said. "Get going."

"Should we position ourselves?" Leo asked.

Sky considered this. It was unusual to have a cluster of people arrive at the fortress steps, let alone five men who seemed put together. Typically, transients arrived as a single person or in a pair, and more typically, they were downtrodden and desperate.

Sky shook her head. "Let's wait. They don't seem to have any weapons and they're not showing signs of aggression."

"Overridden," King said. "I'm going to the roof."

The others stayed at the window while Wyatt went to the double doors and cracked them open, raising his Ruger 10/22 at the strangers on the other side. As he revealed himself, the man who had waved to them crossed the street. He stood at the bottom of the stairs, but did not introduce himself. He didn't appear to be carrying any weapons.

"Can I help you, friend?" Wyatt asked, keeping an eye on the stranger's associates across the street.

"Excuse us. We are only admiring your property," the man said. "You see, myself and my fellow members are looking to relocate and felt this amazing place might suit us."

Members? Charlie can vet this group.

"Well, mister," Wyatt said. "We can't accommodate a group here. We can recommend you to our sister community, the heights, not too far from here. And they can let you know if they have room, if you're interested."

The man smiled. Wyatt noticed the others across the street refocus their gaze upon the roof.

Looks like you got their attention, King.

"We so much appreciate the offer, but maybe another time," the man said. "Thank you."

"What's your name, stranger?" Wyatt asked.

"Vash," the man said before turning around and walking away. Without another word, he led his men down the hill toward the intersection.

Wyatt watched them disappear around the bend before going back inside and shutting the door behind him. King came barreling down the steps from the roof.

"That was quick," King said.

"Yes, he was a man of few words," Wyatt said. "He referred to his buddies as 'members' and said they were looking to relocate, specifically here, and they didn't seem interested in the heights."

"No surprises there," Misty said, departing from the window. "Everyone wants to live here."

"Let's eat cake!" Leo cried.

Each orphan tried a piece of the chocolate cake, concocted by Sky, cooked by Wyatt, and slathered with peanut butter by Leo. They would all admit that it was better than it looked or that they had ever imagined, and the day wore on.

Vash led his men past the intersection and down the street. He followed the road around the bend and stopped when he was out of view of the fortress. His men gathered around him and waited.

"So, what do you think, gentlemen?" Vash asked.

"Did Zagan really die at that place?" asked Mantus, a younger member of the group who they picked from the Temple in Massachusetts.

"That's what our messenger informed us," Vash reminded. "Based on what we just saw, and what we heard, that indeed is the place where Zagan met his death, and it is the place where he shall be resurrected. But not before his enemies have been sacrificed in his name. He would appreciate that, I'm sure."

"The messenger mentioned the heights, too," a member by the name of Balaam said. "We should pay them a visit today as well. We owe them some retribution, and if we can find a weak link there, we may be able to use it to our advantage."

"Do you really think the ritual at his gravesite can bring Zagan back?" Mantus asked.

"Not if you have any doubt," said Pan with a scornful look. "It would be the first time for us, but not the first time in history."

"How ironic it will be to resurrect Zagan on the former grounds of a Roman Catholic church," Vash said. "We'll corrupt its former glory as we bathe in the blood of its protectors. Then, Zagan will make his return."

"He should have never come back here alone," Balaam said. "Had he been more patient and waited for our journey to come full circle, he might have survived."

Vash took in a deep breath. "It was too tempting for him. You must understand, Zagan was a bit impulsive. That's who he was, but he was right to set his sights on that place. It called to him, as it calls to us now. And anyway, Zagan *did* survive. He's waiting for us to finish what he started, and he shall be a powerful revenant."

"*Ave Satanas*," Pan uttered.

"And what about Valley Hall?" Amon asked.

"It's time to move on, my friends," Vash said. "Valley Hall is thirty years past its prime, and the land is losing its sacredness, even with Ms. Betty's attentiveness. It's isolated, and no place to grow our membership back to what it was, in this new age." Vash took two steps toward the fortress and gazed down the desolate road. "Here. Here is where we need to be. It's all connecting. It's ordained."

"So, then," Balaam said. "If Zagan, in all his wild craziness, couldn't take it, how do we?"

Vash smiled deviously. "Cleverly. You see, Zagan was militaristic in his approach. From what we've heard, his tactics to clear the fortress were focused on forceful eviction, and it didn't work. The people in there...they're fighters. And while inside together, they have the advantage from the rooftop to the ground. So, we change tactics. We turn the knife slowly. We make them come out to us, and when they do, we eliminate them, one by one."

"*Ave Satanas*," Balaam said.

"So, we're staying close, then?" Mantus asked.

"You are," Vash said. "Along with Balaam and Amon. I will pay a visit to this 'heights' community while Pan returns to Valley Hall for Ms. Betty. We'll need her. When we are together again, it will begin. We will break their bodies and their spirits. And when they are gone, we will grow our membership stronger than it ever was, and we will be whole again."

"*Ave Satanas*," they all said in unison.

Two

Charlie came down from the heights for the weekly committee meeting, which was held in the library on the second floor. Though the children were always ecstatic to miss some of their school lessons on meeting days, Sky kept them busy anyway with extra chores.

Committee members Charlie, Wyatt, King, Sky, and Misty sat about the circular table in the library as the meeting began. Charlie stashed his flask into the pocket of a green Army fatigue jacket he had worn for years, even though it was showing its age.

"What's the word, Charlie?" King asked. "How are the heights treating you?"

"I'm sometimes weary, my friend, and other times encouraged," Charlie said.

"The story of all our lives," Wyatt said.

"I have a few things on the agenda for today's meeting," Sky proceeded. "I put our strange visitors from yesterday at the top of the list."

"What made these visitors stranger than any others you've come across and sent our way?" Charlie asked.

"It's hard to say," Misty said. "Just a kind of feeling. It almost seemed liked they were probing us, in a nonviolent way."

"They didn't say anything?" Charlie asked.

"The one guy came forward," Wyatt said. "An older guy with a white crew cut. He said they were looking to relocate, and when I mentioned the heights, they just kind of wandered off. Said they would think about it."

"Were they armed?" Charlie asked.

"Nah, they weren't armed," King said. "If they were, we would have vetted them accordingly."

"Where were they relocating from?" Charlie asked.

"I didn't ask," Wyatt said.

"It might have been helpful, Wyatt," Charlie said.

"In retrospect, you're probably right," Wyatt conceded. "But I guess everyone who shows up here is relocating from somewhere."

"A day in the life," King said. "Maybe we should have invited them in for some of Baby's birthday cake."

Misty laughed. "They gave us no reason that would justify torturing them."

"It was a good cake!" Wyatt said with a huff.

"As always, keep your eyes open," Charlie said. "If they return, weapons or not, treat them as hostiles."

"Noted," King said.

"Moving on," Sky said. "Second on our agenda is regarding the slowly paced scouring missions for brick. We need to finish this perimeter wall. Half of a perimeter wall is not cutting it."

They had started to build the perimeter wall, along with other repairs to the fortress, only days after Sim was killed. They had plenty of concrete mix on hand but had to haul brick from near and far to get the wall started. It was an exhausting effort, but once done, the wall would be six feet high and surround the fortress from the street side to the rear, just beyond Usland and Restland.

"Now that the weather is warm, we can get back at it," King said. "These are weird seasons we're having. It was freezing cold all winter and into the longer days of spring, and now it feels like summer, even though it's likely only beginning of May."

"We can probably kick into full speed now and have it done by the time the weather turns cold again," Wyatt said.

"I'll get some men from the heights to help with the hauling," Charlie said.

"Sounds good," Sky added. "Now, can we discuss a roof sniper? We haven't had a consistent person at the job since Shark was killed. It puts us in a vulnerable state, not to always have someone on that roof."

"I still think Skinny Jim was the best candidate for the job," Wyatt proposed.

King sighed. "Skinny Jim nearly shot Teddy, thinking he was an intruder. And if Skinny Jim had done that, I would have murdered him in the worst possible way and tossed his Skinny Jim carcass over the side of the roof."

"He had only known you all a day," Charlie said in his defense. "He has served the heights well. Though he is a little eccentric, he is a great shot; and he is loyal...almost to a fault."

Sky rolled her eyes.

"All in favor of giving Skinny Jim another chance," Wyatt proposed.

"Keeping in mind that using him as our resident sniper means he has to move in," Sky said, eyeing King and Misty in particular.

Misty raised her hand with a bit of discomfort. "At least we know him...somewhat."

The only one that did not vote for Skinny Jim's return was Sky, but she was overruled.

"Fine, then," Sky said.

"I know we have brought this up before, but given the circumstances, maybe it's time to look at it again," Charlie said. "We all know by now why you were brought here by Sim, instead of the prison or some other, more ideal fortification, of which there are at least a dozen in this immediate area. But now that Sim is gone, and this wall construction is taking twice as long as envisioned, maybe it's time to simply use the fortress for its most realistic purpose: as a processing outpost to keep an eye on incoming traffic from the interstate, and as a production plant, instead of using it as a residence."

"Never," King said. "This is my home and where the only family I ever knew lived and died." King dug his index finger into the table. "This family will not leave, and I thought we agreed the topic was never to be put up for a vote."

Charlie looked to the other committee members for rescue. Wyatt made no comment while Misty refused to make eye contact, instead opting to stare at the table.

Sky put her hand on his arm. "I'm with you, King, but remember when you left here all on your own? There may come a time when the others make their own choices about where they go in this world."

King turned to her. "They can go wherever they please when they are old enough. For now, they stay at the fortress."

Just then, King's walkie talkie crackled. "Are we cleaning out Sim's closet today?"

It was Leo.

King rolled his eyes and raised the walkie to his lips. "No, Leo. We've been over this. We are doing that as a family, and today is not the day, least of all when we are in the middle of a committee meeting."

"It's been seven months!" Leo said.

Sky had relocated to Sim's former first-floor bedroom shortly after the battle with Zagan, and though she re-envisioned it to her taste, she stopped short of interfering with the closet, noticing that he had it cluttered with many things, presumably remnants of his former life. Sky promised they would go through his personal belongings as a family. But to date, they had not done so.

"Go gather food from the garden, for crying out loud. And don't hide it in a ditch. Bring it to the house."

"Alright, already," Leo said. "Jeez."

"Over and out," King said.

"What's next?" Misty asked.

Sky skimmed her notes. "We still have not recouped the full arsenal we had before the battle with Zagan," she noted. "We depleted it by thirty percent and only brought back about ten percent from that time. So along with hauling brick, with the warmer weather we should focus our scouting missions on finding weapons, even if it means going further than we ever have."

"We might have to find quicker ways to get places," Misty said. "Other than the shoe-leather express. Especially if we need to go further."

"Well, cars are no good," Charlie said. "Believe me, I have checked several of them. The gas is bad and most of the vehicles out there are mechanically unsound after all these years of decay."

"What about horses?" Misty suggested. "I know how to ride, and I can train others. I had horses on my farm."

"If you're fixin' to ride horses, I can surely help with that. They didn't call me 'Wild Wyatt' back in the day for nothing."

"Oh…" Sky cringed. "Is that what they called you?"

"I've not seen a horse in years," Charlie said, before Wyatt could answer. "Then again, I haven't left the heights in years except to come here."

"I've seen them on runs," King said. "It's a good idea, Sky. Something to consider, anyway. If not now, then in the future."

"All in favor of tracking down, training, riding, and stabling horses, raise your hand," Sky said with an air of sarcasm.

"Well, when you say it like that," Misty said. "It does sound a little far-fetched."

Still, three out of four members of the committee voted yes on a possible horse-finding adventure, Charlie and Sky being the hold outs.

"Go figure," King said. "The ones who actually do the majority of scouting missions want horses, and the commanders in chief of the settlements don't."

"That's true politics," Charlie acknowledged. "But it sounds like horses won."

"A final note," Sky said. "We just need a weekly heights report."

"We are at two hundred and thirteen occupants now," Charlie stated proudly. "We've opened two more buildings on the compound, and in spite of smaller issues that some of my constituents complain about, we are doing well with production, weapons, first aid, and training."

"What about those two rabble-rousers?" Sky asked. "The ones with the weed farm?"

Charlie scoffed. "They drive me crazy...but they are good people. The harvesting of marijuana is for trade purposes only, though there is some disagreement about this. Only ongoing community meetings at the heights will dictate the future of that controversy."

"One big happy family, eh?" King said.

"You know it," Charlie said.

"Okay, then," Sky announced. "Is that it for today?"

"I hope so, because I need a drink," Charlie said.

Sky peered at him with her with a squint. Charlie offered her a sly smile.

Sky regarded the committee and nodded. "Meeting adjourned."

Three

THE NEXT MORNING, THE fortress was bustling with action as the orphans scurried to and fro, organizing their bed covers, bringing down their laundry, and going about their usual routines laid out by Sim years ago. Baby added the hashmark to the "days gone by" wall while Leo opened the shutters. JZ, Teddy, and Misty conducted an outdoors check. King did a perimeter scan from the rooftop with his binoculars.

Sky set the table for breakfast, with the help of Miracle and Yamil, and Wyatt waited on the side porch for Skinny Jim, who was slated to have an interview with King and Sky.

As Sky was setting plates on the table, Leo came around the corner with a big yawn and a stretch. "God, I can hardly get any shut eye with Teddy talking and crying in his sleep over missing his mother all the time. I think I get more rest on guard duty. I'll have to start sleeping in the day."

"Funny," Sky said. "I've been thinking of my Uncle Mike a lot since Sim died. I think Sim's death has set us all back emotionally." She turned to Leo. "Do you think about *your* parents more since Sim died?"

"Not really," Leo said. "My mother tried to kill me."

"Hmph," Sky pondered. "Well as long as you're awake, you can help me set."

Miracle and Yamil laughed and pointed at him as she handed him cups to pass out for the orange juice.

"Why don't you ever make those two do anything?" Leo asked. "They're spoiled rotten. They probably slept like logs all night."

"Don't you know anything about the last-born children?" she cocked her head. "They're always spoiled."

Leo shook his head while adjusting his glasses.

"I have a toothache," Teddy said as he entered the dining room unannounced. "It hurts. It keeps me up at night."

Leo and Sky looked at him. Sky smiled uncomfortably, though she was trying to be reassuring. "Mrs. Chandler was a dental assistant for many years, so we will get you to the heights and let her handle it. We have plenty of medicine to stave off infection, but unfortunately, these days, in many cases decayed teeth must be uncomfortably removed. If it's a small cavity, we may be able to avoid that, so hope for the best."

"If we have to, I can tie a string around it and then put the other end around a doorknob and slam it shut!" Teddy swooped his arm in a grand motion.

Sky patted his head. "That's typically a strategy deployed only when the tooth is loose. Thankfully, cavities in this group are rare, since we are all smart about what we eat and drink. But I'm sure at the heights there is someone seeing Mrs. Chandler every day."

"Speaking of food, can we have the Ramen noodles tonight?" Teddy rubbed his hands together feverishly.

"Is it the seventh day from the last Ramen dinner?" she asked.

Teddy's eyes rolled in his head. "I think only four."

"Then you have three more days," she said. "But you can enjoy johnny cakes with us for now."

"Yippee!" he yelled.

Sim and the orphans had gathered up Ramen noodles by the case, and half their supply closet was Ramen, which had a shelf life of thirty years.

But Sim had only allowed it once a week, as a sort of treat, kind of like the family pizza nights of old.

The family gathered around the table, and together with heads bowed, recited the prayer to St. Michael.

Defend us in battle.
Be our defense against the
wickedness and snares
of the devil.
May God rebuke him,
we humbly pray,
and do thou,
O Prince of the
heavenly hosts,
By the power of God,
Thrust into hell Satan,
And all the evil spirits,
Who prowl about the world
Seeking the ruin of souls
Amen

"And for all those loved ones who were laid to rest in Usland. Let us not forget."

As the family dined on johnny cakes, fruit, and juice, there was relative silence. Leo noticed this quietness and could not be sure where it stemmed from but thought to create conversation. "Can we go to the creek today for swimming?"

"Yay!" Teddy said, raising a fork in the air.

"It's not summer, you know," Sky said. "Although, it seems to be unseasonably warm for May."

"How do you even know it's May?" Teddy asked.

"It's easy when you analyze the hashmarks on the living room wall and connect it to the month when everything went down," Leo said.

"Plus, knowing the number of sunlight hours we have helps," Sky said. "Anyway, speaking of swimming, it's a bath night for the girls. So don't forget, ladies."

The orphans took baths every other night, rotating between boys and girls. The girls always required the water to be warmed over fire before being put into the tub, whereas the boys were fine with cold baths if only to get the process out of the way. Suffice it to say, girls' bath night was a bit more involved.

"I want to go swimming, but you never searched for a proper bathing suit for me like you promised," Baby whined. "The one from last year is too small. I'm at least ten now, you know."

Teddy snorted with a laugh. "Well, you're just lucky the world came to an end when they were selling summer clothing, or you would have to swim in snow pants."

"We'll go up the hill to the plaza when the timing is right," Sky said. "But for now, you can squeeze into the old one. Before we go anywhere, though, we have a family meeting to attend directly after breakfast."

The orphans moaned.

Miracle slapped his forehead. "No meeting."

"Not another one," Baby whined. "Sim had them every month; now we have them, like, every day."

"I don't know what you're all talkin' about anyway," JZ said. "You aren't getting me into that nasty creek water with all those fish and dirt and other disgusting stuff."

"I'll hang tight here at the fortress with anyone who wants to stay," Wyatt said. "I'm not much for jumping in creeks, myself."

"You're from the south," King said. "I thought all you guys did down there was fish, hunt, farm, ride bulls, and jump in creeks."

"Where in the hell do you get your information from, boy?" Wyatt said. "It just so happens, we do much more than that."

"How the hell did you even end up in New York, anyway?" King asked as he was about to stuff a full johnny cake into his mouth.

"How else?" Wyatt said as he gazed upward. "A woman. Sweet Josephine."

"That's a funny name," Yamil said.

"Yeah, really funny," Miracle echoed.

"All right, all right," Wyatt said. "Anyway, Josephine was my girl for two whole months, until she fell in love with a bouncer at one of the bars I took her to. But I never went home, despite my heartbreak. I guess I got used to being a Yank."

"She put up with you for two months?" Sky said with a smile. "She must have liked your cologne."

"What cologne?" Wyatt said, an air of confusion on his face.

"Had she only seen how you slurp up your Ramen noodles," King said, "she might have stayed longer."

"Or maybe not so long," Wyatt said, stabbing at a johnny cake.

"Well, if we are venturing to the creek," Sky said, "then how about we skip a formal meeting and discuss things at breakfast while we eat."

"Sounds good to me," JZ said. "We need more hair and nails stuff, along with razors and sharper cutting scissors too, if I'm going to keep pampering everyone around here. I've had the same hair-cutting scissors that I brought with me from my auntie's shop when I left with Sim. These boys haven't had a cut in over a month, and some of them are getting ready to shave."

Teddy and Leo massaged their chins, looking for hair.

"We'll put these things on our list and get them when we go out on another supply run," Sky said. "Aside from this, at our committee meeting we set upcoming goals, which include scouring for more brick, finding horses, as well as more weapons. The warmer weather is here, finally, so it's time to get back out there and get back to work. Real work."

"Don't sound so happy about it," Teddy said. "I hate hauling bricks. It sucks."

"Language," Sky cautioned.

Leo raised his hand as if he were at school.

"Just speak, Leo," Sky said.

"I think Yamil and Miracle can pitch in with the brick hauling and missions now. They're old enough. We can't baby them forever, and they get away with doing nothing."

"Hey," Yamil said.

"Yeah," Miracle offered. "No fair."

"Don't talk to me about fair, you little turd," Leo said. "You guys sit around here all day and don't even have to set the table, while we have to haul bricks, and now we have to lasso horses."

"Okay, Leo, settle down," Sky said, eyeing the little ones lovingly. "We'll look at ways to get them more involved, but I'm still not sure the timing is right for them to be running missions in the world. Their time will come." She looked around the table. "Did we cover everything from yesterday, guys?"

Sky passed glances between Misty and King.

"You forgot to tell them about Skinny Jim coming back," Misty said.

"He almost killed me!" Teddy said. "Are you serious? If it wasn't for Gigi, I would have been toast."

Gigi heard her name and poked her head up from where she was lying on the floor waiting for someone to feed her table scraps.

"We're going to meet with Skinny Jim," Sky said. "We'll make sure he is on his best behavior, and it'll put someone on the roof all the time, so we don't have to worry about anyone sneaking up on us."

"I miss Shark," Baby said.

There was a short silence.

"We miss a lot of people," Sky reminded. "But, so that we don't have to miss more of us, we need to make sure security remains tight."

With that said, breakfast ended.

"He's here, Sky!" Wyatt said. "Yeehaw!"

"He's only two hours late," Sky said as she joined Wyatt on the side deck and watched Skinny Jim approach. He was wearing a white T-shirt tucked into blue jeans and had a dark pair of shades covering his eyes. He kept his head shaved, and the orphans nicknamed him "Bush Baby" on account of his big ears that stuck out like satellite dishes. He was tall and lean and walked like a Daddy Long Legs.

When Miracle and Yamil met Skinny Jim for the first time, Sky had just finished reading *Jack and the Beanstalk* to them, and they ran away in fright. Skinny Jim had no clue and could only shrug.

Usually, little kids like me.

Today, Skinny Jim was carrying a sack over his shoulder and was sucking on a blade of yellow grass.

"He looks like a giant-sized version of Tom Sawyer," Sky said as he made his final approach to the steps.

When he arrived at the bottom of the stairs, he stopped and smiled through his big teeth. "Well...Skinny Jim is back," he said. "I knew you guys would miss this charming personality before long."

Sky rolled her eyes without saying a word and retreated indoors. Skinny Jim cleared the five steps up to the porch in one giant leap and followed her and Wyatt inside, where Gigi met him with a furious bark.

"Calm down, girl," Sky said.

Skinny Jim put up his arms in defense. "Whoa, girl. Not again. Most animals don't react to Skinny Jim with so much hostility."

Sky looked over her shoulder. "I'm sure she still remembers when she had to stop you from shooting Teddy to death."

Leo and Gigi had been with Skinny Jim on the second-level roof surveying the area when Skinny Jim saw Teddy visiting Flip's grave in Usland.

Holy shit we got a perp, twelve o'clock!

Skinny Jim raised the rifle and nearly squeezed the trigger until Gigi barked and bit his leg, distracting him from the shot.

That's Teddy, you dumbass!

Skinny Jim returned to the heights that same day.

"It sure enough was not one of my finest moments," Skinny Jim offered. "But you don't know that I would have taken the shot. I was going to get a good look through the scope before I fired, but the mutt didn't give me a chance."

"Take it easy on that 'mutt' stuff," Wyatt said through pinched lips.

"That 'mutt,' as you call her, has done far more for the fortress than you have, and is held in the highest regard, as she fought in battle and was the fur baby of our fallen brother, Big Will."

"Her name is Gigi," Teddy said as he entered the kitchen.

Skinny Jim turned to him. "Oh, hey there, little man. I remember you. You're that twitchy little fella."

Teddy could only surmise that Skinny Jim was referring to his eye tic that was more than apparent.

Teddy smiled and humbly declined to retort, acknowledging ignorance as a big part of Skinny Jim's M.O.

With Gigi settled and the others preparing for an afternoon swim at the creek, Skinny Jim and Sky met King in the library. Wyatt also joined them, while Misty, typically involved in such affairs, was assigned to kid-watching.

They seated themselves around the table. Skinny Jim, still munching on his grass, kicked back and put his feet on the table while the others looked on, aghast.

"What's the matter with you, boy?" Wyatt asked. "This ain't the heights, so put those feet down and act like a civilized human. Charlie provided you with a high endorsement, so don't embarrass him."

Skinny Jim immediately withdrew his feet from the table. "Sorry, fellas. It's just, Skinny Jim isn't used to this level of formality."

"How 'bout you stop referring to yourself in the third person, too, while you're at it," King said.

"The third who?" Skinny Jim said.

Sky sighed. "Wyatt, I don't know if this is going to work. Isn't there anyone from the two hundred other people who might take this position more seriously? The rooftop is our first line of defense against intruders. We need this role fulfilled with a competent—"

"Now hold on there, ma'am," Skinny Jim said, suddenly appearing more serious. "Skinny Jim isn't a fool. It just so happens that before I found the heights, I lived in a building annex for months trying to stay alive with my father, auntie, and sister." His eyes changed direction as he recalled the past. "My mother was the only one who died of the plague. Don't know how three of us survived in a single family, but we did. I was so happy. Everyone else...lost everyone else. But then I learned the plague...wasn't the end. It was only the beginning." He looked back at Sky, King, and Wyatt. "The plague was the easy way out. When a gang found our annex...Well, the horrors can't be described as a simple bedridden coughing fit and mucho fast deterioration. These horrors that took the rest of my family...shall never be retold by these lips, because to tell it means to face it." Skinny Jim teared up and swallowed hard. "I can't face it. But what I do know is that people that would do others harm like that...I won't hesitate. Maybe with Teddy, I reacted on impulse remembering..."

"It's okay, Jim," Sky said.

Skinny Jim smiled. Maybe he hadn't heard his name in isolation since the fall. "That's what I like about this place…We're real people here. Not characters. I know what happened with Zagan. It's legendary. I will fight like that. I will protect you. I will die to make sure what happened to my family never happens to anyone in this place." Skinny Jim grabbed Sky's arm over the table and offered a hard stare. "I promise."

Sky nodded.

"Now that's the young man Charlie knows," Wyatt said.

Skinny Jim laughed as he wiped tears from his eyes with the end of his shirt. "I am skinny, aren't I?" he laughed.

Everyone did.

"Maybe you're even more than that," Sky said. "A fortress, perhaps, but I hope we won't need to put your passions to the test. The roof duty is the most important precautionary measure we can take for the sake of security, but it's isolating, boring, and hella hot in the summer."

"I got it," Skinny Jim said.

Wyatt and King left the room, but Sky caught Skinny Jim before he rounded the corner to leave.

"Jim," she said.

Skinny Jim turned around and waited at the doorway, expectantly.

"I'm sorry about your family," Sky said. "I lost my mother, father, and uncle."

Skinny Jim bowed solemnly.

Sky smiled, remembering them fondly. "I think about them all the time."

"We still got 'em in here, though," Skinny Jim said, pointing at his chest.

"We sure do," she said.

Seconds later, Skinny Jim was gone, headed to the roof for a long day's work.

Four

As Skinny Jim took to his post, Sky, Misty, JZ, Baby, Teddy, Leo, Yamil, and Miracle headed for the creek, located a quarter mile beyond the rear boundaries of the fortress. King and Wyatt, remained at the fortress.

Sky brought along the AK-47, formerly used by Big Will, and led the way across the green grasses, past the fruit trees and garden, pausing a moment at the location where Sim died and regarding the flowers left to mark the spot. The other orphans formed a circle around the bouquet, never able to simply walk past without acknowledging him. Teddy waved and yelled up to Skinny Jim.

"It's just me!" he said with a laugh. "Don't shoot."

Skinny Jim gave him a thumbs up.

"We should have just made an exception and buried him here, where he fell," Leo said.

"He would have wanted to be with his wife and child and everyone else," Sky said with melancholy before leading the troop onward.

They followed happily, for the most part, each with a towel slung over their shoulder. Teddy was rubbing his cheek to soothe his pesky toothache, Misty was humming, and Miracle and Yamil were holding hands while they bobbed along. In the front, Sky held her weapon in the ready position, poised to shoot any threat that presented itself. JZ had her axes at the ready, tucked into her waistband as she held the rear.

Remember children, when you are out and about, always use line formation. Someone should have point, and someone else rear. Communicate with hand signals and be stealthy. Know what is coming before it gets here, and never take anything for granted.

JZ didn't want to come, as she didn't swim, but Sky asked her to join for the comfort of added numbers. JZ liked any excuse to wield her axes. Sky was sure she would take down a deer with one of them before their trip was through.

As they reached the edge of the property, they entered the trees, and the overhead sun cut away, though it continued to cast its rays in sharp lines that cut through the cracks in the natural canopy above them, which was formed by mighty oaks and wispy willows.

Misty noted Sky's emotional detachment from the group and pulled up alongside her.

"You don't seem yourself today," Misty said. "I could have led this excursion, you know."

"I'm fine," she said. "It's just, when Leo mentioned Teddy dreaming about his mother, it got me thinking even more of my Uncle Mike. Ever since Sim passed away, there has been a void for me. I enjoyed arguing with him and driving him crazy, but I also loved him, and that distracted me—for a time. But truth is, I think about that day my uncle and I separated more now than ever. It stays with me."

"You said he lived through the plague, but you guys were split up?" Misty recalled. "Do you think maybe he's still alive?"

They entered a clearing, which led to a path carved through the dense fields full of thorny bushes, tall grass, and fallen trees.

"I don't think so," Sky said. "He knew where I was going. He's the one who gave me the map. Had he survived, he surely would have come to find me. But still, sometimes I feel like...maybe he *could* be alive. Somewhere."

"What happened?" Leo chimed in.

Sky slowed her pace along the path. "Truth is...I don't know. We were spotted by a group who meant to do us harm. My uncle kissed me on the forehead and told me to run just before he stole their attention to steer them away from me."

"So, what did you do?" Leo asked.

"I ran," Sky said. "The other way, and I never looked back. I was too scared."

"I would have been too," Misty said.

"I wouldn't be now," Sky said. "I would not have left him. I might have been afraid, but I would have fought. And whatever happened, it would have happened while we were together. I wanted to shoot those men the minute we saw them. It was my uncle who didn't want to get in a fire fight. He was like Sim. Just worried about me being safe all the time."

"He loved you," Misty said. "That's why. Just liked Sim loved all of us."

"Maybe one day you can find him," Teddy added from behind. "Not like me. My mother for sure is gone."

Sky had wondered about the fate of her uncle since the day they split. Could he still be out there? Would he show up on the doorstep of the fortress one day? And if he did, would she recognize him?

"I hope that if he is, he has found a place like the fortress and is king there," Sky said.

As she said this, she veered off the narrow dirt path, and the group left line formation and scrambled the remaining ten yards to the creek bank. The boys cast their shoes, shirts, and towels haphazardly about while the girls found a fallen tree and neatly laid their towels over it.

Seconds later, Leo and Teddy were splashing and having fun. The water was only waist high at its deepest point, which was perfect for Yamil and Miracle, both small in stature and light enough that even the weakest current would whisk them away. They preferred to stay in knee-deep water and splash each other while ferociously giggling.

Misty and Baby tiptoed in, warning the older boys not to splash them, while Sky and JZ sat, legs dangling, at the middle of fallen tree which served as a bridge from one side of the creek to the other. They watched the swimmers in quiet, until nature called.

JZ stood up on the log and raised her arms to form the letter T in order to keep her balance as she traversed the thick trunk back to the creek's edge.

"Stay close," Sky warned.

"A girl needs her privacy, you know," JZ explained, sassily crooking her neck. "So you know where I'll be."

She leapt from the fallen tree onto the creek bank, five steps from where Miracle and Yamil were wading. Miracle splashed some water on her and laughed through his toothless grin. JZ raised a pointed finger at the boy.

"I'm gonna get you, boy," she teased.

Miracle laughed while pushing his dampened black hair away from his eyes with both hands. He normally had his hair tied in a ponytail, but JZ had decided that he should let it hang freely that day since they were only going to the creek.

JZ smiled as she turned away and headed through the brush. She knew exactly where she was going: Fatty Rock. The orphans referred to it as such ever since the day they discovered the distinctive boulder in the middle of the field with the words, *Fatty Rock,* spray painted on it in a crooked black font. They held the boulder in high regard, and the gigantic stone was even a days-gone-by story noted on their wall.

It was a short distance from the swimming hole. All the orphans used it as their choice location when doing their bathroom business in the field. It also made for a nice place to relax, with seating across the top for up to six people.

JZ quickly pushed through the shrubs, vines, and tree branches, and as she arrived at Fatty Rock, she did a double-take and immediately snatched the axe from her waistband. She nearly screamed, until she realized the person sitting on top of the rock looked far from threatening. He was no more than eighteen, with sandy brown hair that looked freshly washed, soft features, sparkling blue eyes, and an athletically sound physique wrapped in a thin white tank top and blue jeans.

He raised his hands in a defensive manner as soon as he saw JZ, but he didn't look scared.

JZ felt her heart racing, and she couldn't be sure if it was because she was scared, or if it was because she was twitterpated. Still, she held firmly to her axe, prepared to throw it as she screamed for help, but she thought to assess the situation more fully first. She could still hear the others a short distance away, splashing around, laughing, and having fun under the glow of the afternoon sun.

"Please don't kill me," the boy said, his voice soft and gentle.

"Who are you, and where the hell did you come from?" JZ asked, her chest heaving.

"I was just enjoying a rest on the rock," he said. "I'm passing through, is all. I'm sorry I frightened you."

"You surprised me," JZ said. "You didn't frighten me. If I were frightened, you would be dead already."

"I can understand that," he said. "You're well prepared to defend yourself, I can see. You know how to throw an axe?"

"I could hit you between the eyes from here," she said, lips pursed.

"I believe it," he said. "Maybe you can teach me sometime."

"Teach you?" she said. "Man, I don't even know you. Start talking."

"I told you I was only passing through," he said. "I came from Schenec-tady. Been there for years, but finally decided I needed a fresh start. I wanted to see what else was out there."

"Schenectady? All the way from Schenectady to the middle of this field sitting on our rock on the same day me and my family are here using the creek? Seems too much a coincidence to me."

"I swear," he said. "I don't want any trouble. Especially from no pretty young lady."

"Don't give me that *pretty lady* stuff," JZ said. "I didn't even do my hair or nails today. I look like shit."

"No, no," he said. "I can see you in my mind all done up. It's a nice picture."

"I'm just a kid, you know."

"I thought kids didn't exist anymore," he said.

"You sound like someone I used to know," JZ said, feeling her arm tire from holding the axe over her shoulder. "Someone we killed."

"I'm just saying...I'm only seventeen myself. You can't be much younger than that. Besides, in this world, everyone is older than they are."

"By how many years?" JZ asked, lowering her axe.

"At least five years," he said.

JZ smiled. "Then I'm almost twenty," she said.

"See that," the boy said. "Problem solved. Anyway, in any world we should make the most of our lives even if it means breaking convention."

"So, you're totally alone?" JZ asked.

He made a cross over his heart. "Cross my heart, hope to die. Stick an axe in my eye."

The boy slid his legs out from underneath his body and let them hang over the rock. JZ stayed in her place and scanned the area with several slow turns of her head. Sim had taken them on training operations in the woods plenty of times, and his teachings stuck with her. He would stop them every ten feet and silence them.

When you're out here, listen for signs of anyone else who might be lurking. Branches snapping. Leaves rustling. Feet shuffling.

At that moment, JZ could only hear the others splashing around in the creek.

"It's just me," he said. "I promise."

JZ tucked the axe into her waistband and took a couple of steps forward. "What's your name, then?" she asked.

"Jesse," he answered. "Jesse Thomas Mansfield. JT, for short."

JZ laughed. "That's strange. I'm J'zara. JZ, for short."

"Well, that would be pretty easy to carve into the tree. 'JT + JZ.'" He etched the letters into thin air with his index finger.

"You're awfully sure of yourself, aren't you?" JZ said.

"I like you," he said. "What can I say? I don't run into friendly people very often. Especially not any pretty girls that also know how to take care of themselves."

"I'm one in a million," she said. "You should come meet my family. If you are looking to settle somewhere, we have a place not too far from here where we can send you to. They certainly know how to break away from conventions there."

"Send me to?" JT said. "I'm not the settling type. And anyway, is that not where you also live?"

She stepped closer to the rock. "It's complicated, but no. Where I live is practically a convent. But it's disciplined. Well-oiled. Sometimes suffocating."

"How 'bout you come up and sit with me for a bit," he suggested, patting the stone beside him.

"No," JZ said. "I can't. They'll be calling for me any minute."

"Well then, how 'bout you come back tomorrow night and meet me here," he said. "By then, it'll be a perfect full moon, and you can see it right through that open space."

JT gazed into the sky, and JZ followed his eyeline to the large gap in the trees that opened to a view of the sky.

"It's a beautiful sight," he said.

"I don't know if that's a good idea," JZ said. "There's a reason we travel in packs. It's dangerous otherwise. Once we forget that, we die."

"I would protect you," he smiled.

JZ caught sight of his beautiful blue eyes and the boy smiled. His teeth were pure white, even glistening in the sun. He suddenly jumped off the rock and approached her. "It would be truly special."

JZ, entranced, might have walked away with him then and there if a voice calling for her had not cut through the air.

"What are you doing, JZ?" Sky called.

"I'm coming," she called back.

"Wait," he said. "It was nice meeting you. Tomorrow, I'll be back here watching the moon, in case you change your mind. But I understand if you can't. Times aren't the same anymore."

JZ swallowed hard and nodded. She turned around and left JT standing there. She found another place to pee, and when she returned to the swimming hole and Sky asked her what took her so long, she failed to mention her encounter. Or perhaps she didn't fail to mention it, but only neglected to tell her, for she had already had her heart set on meeting the boy again. She knew that if she had told Sky about JT, it would have caused much alarm. Sky would have likely gone back to the rock and hunted him down.

Her mind raced. The only boy she had ever gotten close with was Mason Brown. It was before the fall, of course, and she attended a junior high school dance with Mason. They had a good time, though she would rather have gone with Jordan Mackie. Jordan would have kissed her. Mason just wasn't there yet.

Then, the fall.

The only boys she had ever known were the other orphans of the fortress, and though she loved them, it was not the same. She couldn't love them the way she always dreamed of loving a boy.

Maybe this would be different.

Maybe this would finally be her chance.

But how safe was it to meet the boy of her dreams under these circumstances?

Risky.

No risk, no reward.

Five

It was quite the full day with swimming, chores, and now the big reveal. Sky had agreed to open Sim's closet, and all the orphans gathered after dinner to see it. They had lived with Sim for three years, and yet there were many more things to be learned about their surrogate father, which they hoped might be revealed after searching through his personal belongings.

Wyatt had opted to give the orphans privacy, though he too was curious at what they would discover, if anything, about the man who took them in and trained them to survive in a new world. He shut the bedroom door and retreated to the rooftop to check on Skinny Jim, who had to be reminded four times during the day to stop coming down to eat, leaving the rooftop abandoned.

His stomach is like a bottomless pit, Sky had remarked.

He's just used to eating whatever and whenever he wants at the heights. Wyatt had said.

He needs to understand that he is not at the heights anymore, and that our protocol on consumption is markedly different.

He'll come around, but I don't think you'll get him to brush his teeth.

King opened Sim's closet door, and it creaked on its hinges. Miracle and Yamil sat side-by-side on Sky's bed while the others crowded the doorway. They stared into the darkened space, wide-eyed.

"What do you think is in there?" Leo asked.

"A monster!" Misty teased.

"There's only one way to find out," King said, pressing on a button to an electric light presumably placed on the wall by Sim at some point. The room was suddenly aglow. The walk-in closet was a shrine of Sim's clothing, hanging neatly from several hangers. On the floor were several plastic totes and several pairs of shoes.

"Yuck," King said. "It smells musty."

"It's probably his shoes," Teddy commented.

The others ignored him as Baby stepped forward and grabbed one of Sim's shirts. "I remember this." She put the shirt sleeve to her nose and took in a breath as she closed her eyes. "It's him."

Baby pulled the shirt off the hook and stole it from the closet.

King went in and dragged the totes out one by one. There were about six of them, and they represented the heart of his closet. Whatever more was to be learned about Sim would be revealed within the totes' contents.

As they went through each one, they noted a meticulousness in his approach, like the way one compartmentalizes each part of their lives in their mind. One bin was from his early childhood and included a baby book that his mother had kept, his christening outfit, work samples and report cards from his elementary school days, pictures of him as a baby celebrating milestone birthdays, birthday cards, small projects, and other memorabilia presumably handed down to him from his own parents.

"Look at this," Baby said, pointing to the top of one of his report cards. *Gabriel Simpson Ford.*

"So now we finally know where the name 'Sim' actually comes from," Sky said.

"Who ever heard of a person's first name being 'Simpson'?" King mocked.

"It wasn't his first name," Teddy said. "It was his middle name, dummy."

"Same thing," King said. "I never heard of that name before."

"What about that cartoon…*The Simpsons*?" Leo said.

"That was their *last* name," King said. "And how do you know about *The Simpsons*? You're too young to know about that."

"Apparently not," Sky said as she continued to rifle through the contents of the bin. "All fascinating if you want to get a glimpse of Sim as a small child. We'll have plenty of time to look at this in more detail later."

In another bin were trinkets and memorabilia from his teen years, including a varsity letter, pins, buttons, a yearbook, pictures, a photo album, and high school notebooks from some of his classes.

"Why did he keep this stuff?" King asked.

"I guess he was the nostalgic type," Sky said.

"I would never have guessed that about him," King replied.

"I think it's sweet," Misty replied. "My mother got sick of trying to store everything I collected or made, so one day she said she would simply take pictures of all my projects, special things, awards, trinkets, and everything else, and just keep a photo album of it all to save space, and that's what she did. I should have taken the album from the house when I left that day with Sim. Maybe on our upcoming journey I'll go back and get it."

"I want to go back to my house too," Teddy said. "I have to."

"I guess we all need a trip back down memory lane," Sky said.

"Well, I don't know about that," King said. "I can't remember the particular car that Sim fished me out of, and I don't even remember where I lived anymore."

"It sounds like the new world is better than the old one…for you."

"Oddly, that may be true," King said.

The third bin they went through contained items from Sim's military and college days, and others held remnants from his teaching days, including a portfolio loaded with class pictures. King grabbed the binder and examined it closely, eyeing a class photograph of Sim next to his charges.

"He looked so different," King remarked.

"I wonder if Charlie is in one of these," Misty said. "Let's see if we can find him."

As some of the children looked through his bin of teaching memorabilia, Sky opened the other bins, which contained pictures of Sim's wife and their daughter, Sara. Sara couldn't have been more than six in any of the pictures. There was one of her on a pony. Sim was standing proudly beside her as she straddled the small horse, his hand supporting her back. He was smiling ear to ear.

"I never saw him smile like that," Teddy said, peering over Sky's shoulder.

Suddenly, Uncle Mike was at the forefront of Sky's mind, once again.

Remember when I took you to the fair, Sky? I let you ride the pony even though your mother was afraid because you were so small.

I shouldn't have left you behind, Uncle Mike.

"Hey, look," Baby said. "It's a journal."

Sky discarded the picture of Sara into the tote and redirected toward Baby as she opened the marble notebook and flipped through it. It was chock full of entries, handwritten by Sim, each dated.

"It looks like he started this a short time before the plague," Baby noted.

"There are more here," Misty noted.

Misty fished into the tote and pulled out five more marble notebooks all containing journal entries written by Sim. She skimmed through one of them, flipping from page to page, slow enough to preview the entries but too quick to read them in full. "It looks like he wrote every day. About the fortress. About us."

"Read us one," Sky said. Baby pulled Yamil and Miracle to the front of the group because they were shorter and would easily get lost. Teddy, Leo, Baby, JZ, and King formed a semi-circle around Misty and Sky.

"Oh," Misty said. "Here's one about you, Yamil."

Sky turned to Yamil and smiled. He, in turn, grabbed Leo's hand, his cheeks suddenly growing red.

Day 29.

I found Yamil today. He was in his mother's lap, and she was trying to spoon feed him applesauce but could barely lift her arm. When she saw me, she looked relieved. Maybe she knew right away I was a friend. Some people say I have friendly eyes, but sometimes people are afraid of me because I have angular features. I once read that rounded faces make people seem more friendly. Or maybe she didn't care, because one way or the other, it meant her burden was over. She dropped the spoon and looked at me with despair and desperation. Yamil took the spoon from her limp hand and fed himself. He never even looked at me. She was able to utter some words and told me his name, which I decided to keep. He was too young to change it himself. I knelt beside her and took her hand. I smiled to make sure she knew that I meant her no harm. I told her I was going to take her child and that I would love him and protect him with other children, and that he would live and grow into a fine young man. A tear rolled down her soft cheek and she squeezed my hand. Gracias...Cuéntale sobre mí. I didn't know too much Spanish, but enough to understand her. I will, I said to her. She passed before my eyes, and I watched the blood drain from her face until she was white. But she looked satisfied. Yamil didn't even notice. I picked him up and pressed him to my chest, and he rested his head on my shoulder. I put my hand on his back, the entirety of which fit into a single palm. He and his mother were a fortress that sad day, and he will live. I believe God has sent me to Yamil, and that he will send me many more children because he knows they are the future of this world, and that only they can restore it.

Yamil's brown eyes widened, and he looked at the entry on the page almost as if to assure himself that it was real and not made up by Misty on the fly.

"Look at that, Yamil," Sky said. "You see how much your mother and Sim loved you?"

He rolled his tongue around in his cheeks then beamed with a glorious smile. "I remember her."

"I can't wait to read the rest," Baby said, pulling one of the books into her chest.

"Me either," Misty said. "We might learn more about him through these than we could ever know when he was alive. He was so focused on *us* all the time that we never truly did get to know who *he* was."

"He was sad, that's why," Teddy said. "For what he did to his daughter. I don't think he wanted to talk much."

"It was tragic," Sky said.

"You all can suit yourselves on that," JZ said. "I don't think it's right reading a man's journal without his permission."

"How are we going to get his permission?" asked Leo.

"Exactly!" JZ shouted. "You should just put these back in the totes with all his little trinkets and souvenirs and leave them be."

"I don't know, JZ," Sky said. "Maybe Sim wrote these journals with the hope that us orphans, along with future generations, would read them and learn about his life and this place. Of course he knew one day he would die and that these books would be left behind. Maybe these books are as much a part of his legacy as us and the fortress."

"Look at how happy the first entry we read made Yamil," Baby said. "When I'm done with this one, I will pass it along."

"I'll start with some as well!" Misty said, grabbing two of the books at random.

"I guess I'll start with the other three," Sky said. "And as for Sim's closet, it is now officially mine. And Sim's things can remain here until the day we build a museum or shrine, where we can put everything on display so that all those future generations will know what he did for us, and what he sacrificed in trying to reestablish order in this broken world."

Sky closed the closet door, leaving those pieces of Sim behind to be forever held. But they were all relieved, because he was still there through all those keepsakes that he had collected to represent the stages of his life.

His presence was alive and vibrant in the air, for he was the fortress, and the fortress was him.

I love you, buddy.

Teddy hears his mother whispering to him from behind her locked door at the old apartment.

Teddy. It's time to come in, Teddy.

Come see me. I'm here waiting.

He walks toward her door slowly and pauses with his hand on the doorknob.

It's okay, Teddy. You can come in now.

Though anxious, Teddy opens the door. She is sitting on the edge of the bed. When she sees him, she holds out her arms, but Teddy cringes because the skin on her face is peeling and worms are sliding in and out of her eye sockets and spiders crawling out of her ears.

I've missed you, Teddy. I'm so glad you're here.

She reaches for him.

Teddy woke with a start. He was sweaty and his heart was pounding. He felt tears run down his face from the corner of each eye. He jimmied off his covers and tossed his legs over the side of his bed and buried his face in his hands. He dreamed about his mother often, more so after Sim died, but they weren't always as unpleasant as that one.

As he wiped the water from his eyes, he saw Leo soundly asleep, awash in the glow of the moonlight that was delicately intruding upon their room. He became aware of his aching tooth again. He reached into his mouth and massaged his gum around the affected area. It was getting worse every day, and he was growing concerned.

Teddy rose from his bed and went to his window, which was fully open to allow for the Spring breeze to enter. As he peered upon the area in front of the fortress, he thought he saw a light moving in the yard behind one of the homes across the street. Teddy rubbed his eyes to make sure he wasn't dreaming, and when he opened them, there were two beams of light, as if there were people out there with flashlights.

Teddy's tooth began to throb, and his heart, which had been slowing down, started to race again.

What would people be doing out there with flashlights in the middle of the night so close to the fortress?

Something was off.

He remembered when Sim taught them to trust their instincts. Sim held an entire session about gut sensations and hair standing up on the back of their necks, and how to act on it.

Why ignore your body when it is telling you in all its subtle ways to either flee or fight?

He grabbed a walkie talkie from his nightstand. He raised it to his mouth and pressed the button.

"This is Teddy," he said. "Skinny...are you out there?"

Skinny didn't reply, but Baby did from the first floor. "What's wrong?"

"You're on watch downstairs?" Teddy asked.

"Yeah, what's wrong?" Baby responded.

"Did someone call me?" Skinny Jim replied.

Teddy kept his eye outside, and the two moving lights went back to being only one moving light.

"It looks like there might be people with flashlights across the street," Teddy said. "You see anything up there, Skinny?"

"I'm on the lower roof scouting the backside," Skinny said after a crackle of the radio. "But I can go up top. Hold on a second."

"Let me look too," Baby said.

In the meantime, Teddy stuck his head out the window and leaned forward as far as he could. He waited for his eyes to adjust to the darkness and held his ear to the street. He thought he saw movement and heard whispering, but like a candle blowing out in the wind, the other light disappeared.

He was spooked when the radio crackled back on. "I don't see anything down here," Baby said. "You said you saw a light?"

"Got nothing from the top with the night vision," Skinny Jim replied. "Not a creature is stirring except an owl in the tree off the lot."

"You were probably just dreaming," Baby said. "Should I wake Sky?"

Teddy considered this as he continued to peer into the yards across the street, as if he could spot something that the night vision goggles couldn't.

Why ignore your body when it is telling you in all its subtle ways to either flee or fight?

"Yes," Teddy said. "Just report it to her as a non-emergency."

Leo rose from his sleep. "What's happening?"

Teddy turned away from the window to address Leo. "I thought I saw some lights out there, but Skinny Jim checked with the night vision and there was nothing."

"Lights?" Leo asked, rubbing the sleep from his eyes. "Like a flashlight?"

"That's what it looked like to me," Teddy said.

"Well, I guess if there was anyone there, the night vision would have saw them."

"Unless they ducked behind a house or something," Teddy said. "It's just weird."

"Even if there was anyone out there, it wouldn't be the end of the world," Leo said. "No pun intended. There are still people out there, Teddy. We're not the only ones."

"No, I know," Teddy said. "But with those strange guys the other day, we should be a little more alert."

"They freaked you out?" Leo asked.

Teddy came and sat next to Leo on his bed. Leo turned his body so his feet were on the floor. He put his arm around Teddy.

"Maybe a little," Teddy said. "But it was more nightmares tonight freaking me out."

"Again, huh?" Leo said.

"And this tooth," Teddy said, cupping his cheek in his hand.

Just then, Sky ushered herself through the doorway of his room. "Baby said you saw a light outside?"

Teddy pointed out the window. "I thought I did."

Sky walked to the window, hunched over, and peered out through the open space into the darkness. She turned back to Teddy a minute later. "I don't see anything."

"Yeah," Teddy said. "Nobody did but me."

Sky took Teddy's radio and put it to her mouth. "Jim, can you keep an extra eye out from the topmost platform with regular night vision scans every fifteen minutes?"

"I sure can," Skinny Jim responded.

"Baby, just keep eyes and ears out, as always," Sky said.

"I can do that," she said. "It's almost King's turn, though."

"When you wake him up, make sure you tell him about what Teddy saw."

"I will," she said.

"Goodnight," Sky said.

After Sky departed, Leo returned to bed while Teddy continued to sit on the edge of his.

Leo must have sensed his anxiousness and said, "You want to sleep next to me tonight?"

Teddy turned to him and smiled. He slid his body beside Leo, and the two fell back to sleep, their heads touching, awash in the light of the moon.

Six

It was a quiet morning, no doubt because of the chaos in the middle of the night.

"For those of you who aren't aware, Teddy said he saw some flashlights across the street when he woke up in the middle of the night." Sky said, looking around the table. "He was concerned there might be people lurking around the fortress, but Skinny Jim cleared the area with his night vision and nobody else saw anything. It remained a quiet night, overall."

"So, then what?" Misty asked.

"Just keep your eyes out for anything that looks off," Sky said from the head of the table before turning to Teddy. "You did good, Teddy. As long as we all continue to work together and remember what we've been taught, one fortress will continue to protect the other."

"Well said," Wyatt offered with a short clap, which drew the attention of the other orphans.

"Really?" JZ offered.

The orphans went back to eating, silently, until Sky offered a table challenge to them in order to redirect their thoughts.

"Let's do a round of Sim Says, shall we?" Sky offered. "Some of his most memorable trainings. Go."

"I always loved the target practice with the Nerf guns," Teddy said.

"His daily exercises to help us build strength, coordination, and stamina," King laughed. "His squats were the funniest."

Pop a squat. Pop!

"Remember the chair challenge?"

"Oh, man," Leo said. "That was hard."

"What on God's green earth was that?" Wyatt asked.

"Sim had us sit in a chair, and he tied our hands behind our back and our feet to the legs," Leo stated proudly. "Then he timed how long it took us to escape."

"Shark had the record on that," King said. "Under three minutes."

"I remember his lessons on how to tell if people were lying," Misty said. "That's how I knew Miracle was lying when he broke the dishes that time."

Miracle slapped his forehead.

"His obstacle courses rocked," Baby said.

"Punching bag," Teddy said.

"What about how to make fire?" Sky said.

"Boring," Leo laughed.

"Booby traps," King said.

"You said 'booby,'" Teddy pointed out.

All the boys laughed, even Wyatt. Sky gave him a look, and he covered his mouth in shame.

"I loved the lesson about the Achilles' heel," Misty said.

"What heel?" Teddy asked.

"Don't you remember, Teddy?" Sky said. "When Sim told us how everyone has a weakness, and that if we are ever in danger with a bad person, we just have to look for their weakness and exploit it."

"What was Zagan's Achilles' heel?" Teddy asked.

"He thought he was smarter than everyone else," Leo said. "He was wrong."

"Okay," Wyatt said. "What about me? Just saying, if you had to take me down, what's my weakness?"

"Uh, you snore," King said.

Some of the kids giggled.

"What's that got to do with anything?" he asked.

"If I was going to kill you, I'd do it while you were sleeping, because you wouldn't hear me coming even if I walked up on you with jingle bells attached to my entire body."

Wyatt shooed him. "Nonsense. I don't snore."

"What's my Achilles' heel?" Sky asked, arms folded.

"That's easy," King said. "The same thing as every one of us sitting at this table. It was Sim's, as well."

"That is?" Sky said.

"Each other," King stated, matter of fact.

The room fell silent.

"Is that good or bad?" Misty asked.

"I guess in the sense that it's easy to determine, it's bad," King said. "Because there will always be someone trying to get at each of us by using the others. With threats, it's not always easy to tell right away what their weaknesses are. So, maybe it's finally time to share one of my days-gone-by stories, since you mentioned Zagan's Achilles' heel. It wasn't just that he thought he was smarter than everyone else. There was something else, too."

The group shifted in their chairs, curious.

"You see...when I left the fortress those months ago...most of you know that I ended up at the heights. But what you don't know...is that I did track Zagan down and confronted him."

Sky tilted her head. "Confronted him?"

"I found him at the prison," King said. "I knew I couldn't blast my way in and expect to get to him before I was gunned down...So I gave up my weapons to have a meeting with him. Face to face."

"Hold them horses," Wyatt muttered. "You did *what*?"

"That's some fool white-boy stuff going on there," JZ said.

Sky ignored JZ's comment and stiffened her posture. "And?"

"I saw a man," King said. "A vile man, at that." King's lower lip trembled. "But he was human. Scarred. I pried him for his story. I wanted to know what led him to this point in his life. I was either going to die there, or I was going to find out more about this man. Or both. I won because I walked out of the prison that day with more information about Zagan than he had ever shared with anyone. I learned he had watched his mother get beat and eventually killed right in front of him. I learned he even killed his own father in return..."

"Go on," Sky said.

King looked at everyone around the table, and then at Sky. "I partly understood his rage."

Sky folded her arms as she regarded him with an accusatory look, recalling that he arrived on the scene of the battle only after Sim had been mortally wounded, and after Big Will, Ace, and Shark had been slain.

"You understood him?" Sky asked, accusingly.

His eyes glassed over. "There's more, though. He let me go on the field out back when we met again. He could have killed me. But instead, he let me go."

"Why?" Misty asked.

King turned to Misty. "I think he was afraid of me. Like I had some power over him in knowing something about his life that even those closest to him didn't know. You see, if we let it, our own trauma can be an Achilles' heel." King looked around the table to each orphan. "Don't let anyone use your past to weaken you. Ever. It's something Sim never taught us, and that we can learn from this story.

A short time later, after they'd finished breakfast and while they were all attending to morning chores, King came through on the walkie from the rooftop. He was replacing Skinny Jim, who was on a morning sleep schedule.

"Looks like we have a visitor approaching," King said. "Doesn't look too serious. An old woman with a shopping cart. She stopped in front, though."

Baby and Misty approached the front doors and opened them to the old woman with the creaky shopping cart. She stopped and hobbled to the stairs.

"Lord, have mercy," she cried. "I heard this is the place to stop if we're looking for sanctuary, but never dreamed I would be welcomed by young children. Have I died and gone to Heaven?"

"Truthfully," Misty said, regarding the woman in her brown frock and brand new pearly white sneakers, "this place is as close as you will get to Heaven, these days."

"Are you carrying any weapons on you or in that cart?" Baby asked, holding her M-16 at the ready.

"Oh, no," the woman said. "I don't like them things. Most people on the road don't bother an old lady like me, so I have no need for them."

Baby walked down the stairs and lifted the tarp on the old lady's shopping cart. She had some canned goods, blankets, a book, and a pillow.

"The name's Ms. Betty," the woman said.

Baby covered the shopping cart back over.

"Well, Ms. Betty, you are welcome to come in, but people don't stay here long term. You can stay a night, and then we'll bring you to the heights community nearby. They'll have a place for you there."

"Oh, you're so kind," Ms. Betty said.

"We have to pat you down, though, before you come in. Baby will move your shopping cart around to the side of the house so it's safe for the night. You won't need anything from there during your stay."

"Hotel treatment," Ms. Betty said. "It's been so long since those days."

Baby got behind the cart and pushed it off while the old woman with greasy gray hair climbed the stairs. When she got to the top, she held out her arms as Misty patted her down. Sky arrived at the door during the processing, and the old woman nodded.

"My name is Sky," Sky said. "Nice to meet you."

Yamil and Miracle came up behind Sky and peered around her curiously.

"Oh, my," the woman smiled. "Aren't you precious. Darlings. I haven't seen so many children in one place since my days in daycare. Whew. What is this place? Some sort of refuge for children?"

"Something like that," Sky said. "Leo will take you around and show you the place, and he will also be your shadow while you are here. We don't allow guests to wander freely in the fortress, nor be alone at any time. I'm sure you understand, and we are sorry if it makes you uncomfortable, but it's protocol. We have dinner when the clock in the kitchen says six. You can sleep on the living room couch tonight, and if you are interested in putting a painted handprint on our welcoming mural, Leo will also assist with that."

"A handprint?" Ms. Betty asked. "What in the world? This is truly special."

Just then, Leo entered the foyer. "Did I hear I got shadow duty?"

"Yes, sir," Sky said. "It's your turn in the rotation, if I recall."

Before Misty could close the doors behind her, Teddy and King passed through.

"Where are you going?" Sky asked. "Aren't you supposed to be on the roof, King?"

"We won't be long," King said. "Just crossing the street to check out the area where Teddy saw those lights last night."

"Hurry up, then," Sky said. "Teddy has lessons."

"Why do you think I chose now to go?" Teddy laughed. "By the way, when am I going to the heights to get this tooth fixed? It's killing me."

Sky patted his head. "Tomorrow."

After she was cleared for entry, Ms. Betty did the tour, added her handprint to the mural, and set up on the living room couch. She insisted on using her own blankets and pillows from her cart, however. Sky radioed King and Teddy to bring her belongings in when they came back.

King and Teddy ventured across the street and peeked in all the neighboring yards, which sloped downward toward the highway and bridge.

"Let's take our time," Teddy said. "I hate math."

"Do you like being dumb more?" King laughed.

"I'm not dumb," Teddy said.

"You will be if you keep ditching your lessons," King retorted as they looked around. "What did you hope to find out here, anyway?"

"I don't know," Teddy said, as he picked up a stick and started swinging it around. "Footprints?"

"Maybe if there was snow or something, but where do you think we'll find footprints?"

"In the dirt, maybe," Teddy offered.

"Well, I don't see anything," King said, steading his weapon, an AR-15. "Maybe it was UFOs you saw, and they were coming to suck you up in their ship and perform experiments on you."

"They'd be more interested in you and your big head and knowledge of chess," Teddy laughed.

"I told you I would teach you," King said. "And stop swinging that stick around before you hit me in my big head."

"Nah," Teddy said. "I can't focus long enough to learn chess."

"I guess you're right," King said. "You're more of an adventurer."

Just then, Teddy dropped his stick and ran over to a load of brick that was sitting alongside the foundations of one of the houses.

"Would you look at that!" he cried. "All this brick has been sitting here the whole time, and we've been traveling all over to find more."

"Go figure," King said. "You can blame the girls for that. They're the ones that said they checked up and down the street and didn't see anything. It's not like it's nearly enough to complete the wall."

"Even one less brick to have to carry from a mile away is better than nothing," Teddy decreed.

"I guess so," King said. "We'll haul them after we get that tooth of yours fixed. For now, let's get out of here. I have to get back to the roof and *you* have to get to your math lessons. Anyway, what you saw last night was probably just that old lady bebopping around while she waited till morning."

The two walked back across the street to Ms. Betty's cart and removed the blanket and pillow to bring to her. Underneath those items, alongside some canned goods, was a flashlight. Teddy and King exchanged looks.

"See, what did I tell you?" King said.

"I guess," Teddy said. "But it doesn't prove it was her."

"Yup," King said. "You're just hoping it was aliens."

"It would be kind of cool for an adventurer like me to go to outer space," Teddy said. "It might even be better than earth."

King scoffed. "A black hole would be better than earth, at this point."

The two walked inside and presented Ms. Betty with her comfort items. She sprawled out on the couch and took an afternoon nap.

The rest of the day and evening were business as usual as the group introduced themselves to Ms. Betty and filled her in on the heights, where they would travel tomorrow.

Seven

WHEN THE MOON REVEALED its full self in the night sky, high above the fortress, JZ tiptoed from her room, careful not to wake Misty. She considered inviting her along so as not to risk going alone, but she didn't want to scare JT off. He seemed so gentle and sincere. She felt safe. It was strange how she could feel this way when she only met him briefly, but sometimes true love started in such ways. An instant connection. A spark. A short conversation.

Or so she had heard. Her mother had always told her that when she met her father, it was love at first sight. They got together when they were sixteen and married four years after.

What was it about Dad that you knew he was the one?

Some boys were teasing me about my braces. I got braces as an older teen. That was an awkward time to have a mouth full metal, let me tell you. Dad stuck up for me and told me my braces were sexy. Because I was sexy. I said, you know what, you're pretty fine yourself. From there, we just...found a connection that thankfully never broke down.

Until the end. They died together in the same bed only two days apart and holding hands. But JZ had learned a lot from them. That true love was possible. It was everywhere. We just had to find it. She had not only observed it in her own parents, but in Sim and her brothers and sisters. She considered herself as lucky as anyone could be, given her life and times.

She carefully crept to the basement after giving Gigi some attention as she lounged in the living room. She wanted to make sure Gigi was comfortable, so she didn't follow her or start barking. She unlocked the doors leading to the underground tunnel, and though she hated the dirt-and-earthworm-smelling corridor that led to the border, she felt it was the best way to break through the perimeter without being detected by Skinny Jim—if the fool was even awake. He didn't seem to take things as seriously as Shark did. But then again, he was from the heights, and Sim hadn't nurtured his sensibilities.

She used a flashlight to carve a visible path to the other end, remembering how hard she worked alongside Leo and Teddy digging the hole back out after it was collapsed by a grenade during the battle with Zagan. It was an entire day's work. Shoveling up mounds of heavy dirt into buckets and heaving the buckets out through the hole. As part of the tunnel's restoration, there came much debate about how it would play into the future plans for the fortress compound.

The new perimeter wall was being built roughly five feet in front of the hole, which many argued about. Some argued that it would make little sense to have the egress tunnel remain inside the compound, because in the event of a real emergency, they would be trapped. But the opposing side argued that leaving the exit to the tunnel outside the wall would make them vulnerable if it happened to be discovered by an outsider, who could then use it to breach the fortress.

The tunnel hole has been exposed to outsiders for the past nearly four years, so there will be no difference if it remains so with strong camouflage.

Yes, but the entire point of the wall is to make our compound more secure, so having an entrance into the compound from beyond the wall makes our efforts moot.

The steel door in the basement is locked at all times, so even an outsider who managed to find his way in could not breach the fortress without heavy explosive power.

How about we lay a bear trap beneath the stairs, so if an outsider comes down, he'll step on the trap!

No doubt one of us would be the one stepping on the trap if it were there.

The debate continued for a long time over many days, but it was ultimately decided that the hole would lead out of the compound. It was the only thing that at least four of the five committee members felt made sense, with King opposing.

JZ shone her flashlight upward, casting the short ladder in a cascading white light. She sighed, thinking about how she would have to push through the barrier, which was covered with earth, sticks, and other debris. She didn't want to be filthy when she met with JT.

She pushed upward with both arms, like Atlas holding the earth above his head. She grunted and growled as the covering slowly lifted. It freed loose dirt from the top, which showered her arms and shoulders. Her lips took on some dirt and she flicked it away with her tongue as she pinched her eyes shut to keep them clear.

With continued exertion, JZ managed to push the plywood flap up and over so that half of the hole was open, which was enough for her to squeeze through. Like a rabbit emerging from its hole, she was free. She glanced at the fortress in the distance after regaining her stance. She was confident that even if Skinny Jim was on the roof wide awake, he likely was not looking through his nightscope in her direction at that precise moment.

She brushed the loose dirt from her jeans, tank top, and arms, and mussed her hair until she was once again presentable. She felt for her axes, which were tucked neatly into the back waistline of her pants, then dragged the plywood square back over the hole. She did not cover it with debris, figuring it would be a dirty hassle to have to uncover it again when she returned.

Slowly, she crept through the rustling trees, her only guide being the moonbeams that cut through the canopy. She did not want to turn her flashlight back on before reaching the clearing, in case Skinny Jim had his eye out.

What are you doing, girl? You're crazy. Absolutely crazy. You're breaking one of Sim's cardinal rules. Remember what happened to Tak and Flip when they went out on their own?

It's fine, girl. You met the boy. He's harmless. Even if he tries to pull something, you can take him down with your axes quicker than he could blink an eye.

What about those strange men that came by the other day? Is it a coincidence that JT showed up at the same time? Remember Kellogg? He was an imposter. Didn't you learn anything?

Tak was only a baby. He couldn't defend himself. You can. And what about Kellogg? He was harmless? A fortress hero. That's what I remember.

As far as those men...they came and left. What would this boy have to do with them anyway?

Be careful.

Be careful.

As she pressed on to the clearing, she tripped a few times over loose stones and tree roots. A branch caught her on the side of the face and tore into her skin. She caressed the scratch, soothing it, and felt a small amount of blood oozing from the wound.

"Damn," she said to herself. She turned on her flashlight, not caring if Skinny Jim saw it. What could anyone do, at that point? As long as the light wasn't approaching the fortress, they would only keep an eye on it anyway. Like with the light Teddy reported seeing. They wouldn't send anyone out into the dark to chase a fleeing light.

She reached the clearing, then the path, and the second part of her journey came with much more ease with the aid of the flashlight. Animals stirred in the brush around her, an owl hooted. But other than that, the night was as dead as the day, but it felt more normal because at night, it was supposed to be dead quiet. Quiet. Daytime in the city was supposed to be loud and busy. But not in these times.

As she approached Fatty Rock, she saw the light of a fire and decided to shut off her flashlight as she pushed through the remaining tree branches. The campfire was alight in front of Fatty Rock, and it cast JT's face in a warm orangish hue. He smiled when he saw her, and she smiled as well, though he probably couldn't see her face so far away from the light source.

"I knew you would come," JT said, his eyes narrowing.

"How?" JZ said. "Am I that predictable after only a five-minute conversation?"

"I just knew," JT smiled. "You looked like the type that would tempt easy."

JZ swallowed hard, and her smile melted simultaneously. "There's nothing easy about me, so what's with the attitude, all of a sudden?"

JT smiled and said, "You're ours now."

I told you. I told you, you dummy. You should have listened!

No risk, no reward.

No reward.

JZ swallowed hard and immediately reached her hands around to the backside of her jeans to snatch up her axes, but her attempts were thwarted by another presence who grabbed them from behind and pushed her forward toward the fire.

JZ spun around and watched as four more men emerged from the forest.

Oh, my God. I know these guys. These are the same hell-ass fools that came to the fortress during Baby's birthday.

Her heart skipped a beat. She turned back to JT, trying to picture him with the others that day when they came seeking relocation. She kicked herself for overlooking it.

You are not a coward. Remember that. You're a fighter.

JZ, summoning up courage even in what might be her last moments, did not intend to cower. She turned back toward JT even though it meant turning her back to the others.

"So, you got me, JT, you genius, because you knew a fifteen-year-old girl would like a boy. But guess what, you aren't even cute. You're just a pathetic chump." She turned around and spit toward the other men who stood by leering. She laughed. "And screw you too, you chicken hawk rejects. Five of y'all assholes against a little girl. Pitiful."

"Talk all you want," said the man who had presented himself as Vash to Wyatt. "Your frustration is understandable because you're trapped, young lady, but our mission is clear. Your people took Zagan from us, and we need his gravesite and your fortress to build back our temple and to resurrect him. It's like killing two birds with one stone, as they say."

JZ turned back to JT, who was standing in the light of the fire, a smirk across his face, infatuated with Vash's words.

"Did you say, 'resurrect him'?" she burst into laughter. "You want to bring Zagan back from the dead?" She laughed some more. "You guys are trippin'. You'll have to bring his ass back without a head because we cut that clean off." She turned to JT. "You must be crazy to be following these half-baked idiots."

JT's smile melted to a grimace. "You know what JZ, I was there at the house the other day. The reasons you didn't truly recognize me at the rock was because you were blinded by your desire, and because my face was clean. I am Mantus, and my face will soon be stained with your blood and the blood of your brothers and sisters. One by one...you will all be cast away. We will make you blind, stupid, and miserable. And then, when it's all done...we will hold a grand bonfire in your backyard, into which we will cast your bodies as Zagan makes his glorious return."

JZ felt her blood surge, though she knew she had to keep her emotions in check, lest they put her at a disadvantage. She had no idea if she was going to live or die, but she did know she was not sacrificing anything. "You don't know us too well, do you, dipshit?"

Just then, she bent over and grabbed a handful of dirt and tossed it over the fire into JT's face. He recoiled as she spun around and threw a solid kick into Vash's stomach. He cried out in pain as he clutched his gut and dropped her axes to the ground. She scooped up her axes deftly as the other men descended upon her. With a fierce snap of her arm, she targeted the closest body part to her...the arm of one of the other men. The blade of her first axe landed true, splitting the skin on one of the vile men's arms. She quickly turned around and hurled the other axe at JT, who was advancing around the fire. The axe landed squarely between his eyes, and he stumbled backward, a look of surprise carved across his soft face. He fell into the fire, and a cloud of embers rose up and danced into the night sky.

She advanced toward the tree line. But before she could make it, she was overpowered by the other men, who tackled her and held her. Vash, quickly recovered from JZ's kick, stood over her as she lay pinned to the ground by the other three men, one of them holding both arms, and the others at each of her feet. One of them was bleeding profusely from the arm that JZ had cut with the axe. His blood oozed onto her right shin and foot, and she felt it trickle down and around to her calf.

It's over now, girl. Was it worth it?

She struggled to move but realized it was futile, so she decided to relax, not yet giving up hope of cutting free from her human bindings...if she could only get one hand free.

She remembered, as a young girl, when her mother set glue traps in their house to capture mice. One day, she saw the results. Three mice were affixed among two glue traps. One was dead, and the second one beside the first was simply sitting, docile, as if it realized its struggles were futile and gave into its fate. The third was trapped by the tail, and one foot was flipping and flopping on the second trap, struggling to somehow get free.

She now understood the mindset of the two live mice, loathe to suffer the same fate as the third.

Don't go quietly. Do everything you can to break free. Never give up.

"Fight, scream, and thrash," Vash said. "We expected nothing less from you."

"JT didn't look like he expected to have my axe buried in his face," JZ said. "But don't worry, you'll join him soon. Matter of fact, why don't you save us all some trouble and just jump into the fire now. Take all these other fools with you."

Unsmiling, Vash said, "You have your God, and we have ours. We'll see who's standing in the end. We at least know it won't be you."

As JZ squirmed, Vash withdrew a twenty-two-inch steel sword from a long brown sheath. JZ felt her eyes widen as it glistened in the moonlight, and she burst into another round of struggle, trying to free herself. One hand. One leg. Please. The men were too strong. Even the grip of the man she had injured was firm.

Vash knelt alongside her waist, sword in hand. He wrapped his hands around the handle and raised the sword above his head. JZ scowled and tightened her abdomen as Vash plunged the blade into her stomach, just beneath her navel. She cried out to the heavens as it pierced the depths of her body. It felt like a punch to her gut. She did not want to give him the satisfaction of her defeat, but she couldn't hide the intense agony.

Vash pulled the blade from her body and cast it aside. He swiped at the blood leaking from her deep wound and covered his hand in it. He flicked the blood onto the faces of the other men who held her, and as the warmth of the red liquid hit their faces, they moaned in ecstasy and released JZ's arms and legs. Vash covered his own face with her blood as JZ curled into a fetal position holding her gut. She spat blood and cried.

All this for a boy. You fool.

You followed your heart, J, and not Sim's trainings. Don't fret. It's human nature. For you will be in paradise soon. With Ace, and all the others.

You could have lived longer if you had not been blinded.

Sometimes we have to risk everything for fulfillment. At least you killed JT. One less the others will have to deal with.

As JZ lay dying, the four men danced around the fire, chanting weird words and reaching out to the skies. She attempted to pull herself into the tree line as they were distracted, but she could hardly move. She made it about five feet on her stomach, clawing and scratching at the ground before Vash grabbed her by her legs and flipped her onto her back. "Don't go too far, my dear," he said.

JZ coughed hard, releasing blood and sputum. "I...want...to tell you something."

Vash smiled, and it was the first time since she had seen him that she had witnessed some emotion from him—it was a perverse emotion, at that. He was proud. "Last words. What can I tell the rest of your family before they die?"

JZ whispered low enough that Vash was unable to hear her. Vash, drenched in her blood, leaned over and put his ear to her trembling lips. JZ seized the opportunity and snatched his earlobe with her teeth and bit down as hard as she could. Vash wailed and tried pulling his body upward, and as he did, JZ's body lifted in kind, as she did not let go until she had bitten off the lower part of his ear. With the piece of rubbery flesh in her mouth, she fell with a thud back to the ground and spit it to the side and laughed wildly, her mouth bathed in Vash's blood.

"You hear me now, asshole?" She laughed some more and realized she felt no more pain.

Vash, holding the side of his head, reached for the sword. And once it was in hand, he swiped it across JZ's neck. The blade opened her neck from ear to ear, and blood spurted several inches into the sky. She spat and sputtered until all the life drained from her body.

She couldn't complain about her choice to meet JT, as she made it of her own free will. Besides, she had already met some of the greatest men to ever live in this new world or the old one. She saw them all in her mind as her life faded to black, and they were beautiful.

All of them.

Eight

WHEN MORNING CAME, THE orphans went about their normal routines. Misty didn't even think it odd that JZ was not in her bed, as she assumed she was already up and about doing her chores. JZ was typically the early bird, of the two of them.

However, when breakfast came and JZ was not accounted for at the table, everyone looked to each other for an explanation. Skinny Jim was shoveling scrambled eggs into his mouth, courtesy of the fortress chickens, and didn't seem to notice the others pondering.

"Well?" Sky said. "Where is she?"

"Who?" Skinny Jim said, not looking up and shoveling scrambled eggs into his mouth.

"Did you see her this morning, Misty?"

"She wasn't in the room when I woke up," Misty said. "Her bed was not made."

Misty hadn't thought of it before then. If JZ had gotten up, she would have most certainly made her bed before leaving the room. It was her habit.

"Anyone?" Sky said, glancing around the dining room table.

"Could she be in the outhouse?" Wyatt asked.

"King, can you check it out?" Sky asked. "Everyone up. Breakfast is on hold until we find her. Leo, to the third floor. Misty, to the second. Teddy, check the basement. Yamil and Miracle go to the living room and wake Ms. Betty. Maybe she can assist us."

"What do you want *me* to do?" Skinny Jim asked.

"What were you asked to come here to do?" Sky asked.

"On it," Skinny Jim replied, dropping his fork, and dashing to the rooftop for a scan.

Baby joined Misty, while Yamil with Miracle roused Ms. Betty and Wyatt checked the outhouse. The group reconvened in the kitchen once they checked their respective areas.

"What's all the fuss?" Ms. Betty asked, stretching her arms with a yawn as she entered the kitchen behind the little ones.

"One of us has gone missing," Baby said.

"Oh, my," Ms. Betty declared.

Teddy was the last one to report, and when he did, he wore an ashen face.

"What?" King asked.

"The door to the tunnel is wide open," he said. "She left."

"Left?" King pushed past Teddy and ran to the basement. The others followed.

"What the hell did she do?" he muttered when he saw the opening to the tunnel. "Meet me out there."

King dashed ahead and ran into the tunnel. Teddy followed. Sky and the others ran back up the stairs and across the compound to the other end where the tunnel let out. King had beat them and was standing at the mouth of the foxhole.

"When do you suppose she left?" King asked.

Sky jumped on her radio. "Jim?" she said. "You copy?"

After a bit of snap and crackle, Jim responded. "What's up down there? I see you guys."

"You didn't see anything last night, though, or prior to breakfast out here? Nothing strange? Movement? Light?"

Sky briefly thought of the night previous, and Teddy's report.

"It seemed quiet to me," he said. "Although it's hard to tell outside of the regular scans with the nightscope. What's going on, anyway?"

Sky lowered the radio without a response. She didn't want to wear panic on her face, but she was afraid for JZ. She tried to imagine the circumstances under which JZ would have left. Alone. It was one of the biggest violations of protocol.

"We ought to go look for her," Wyatt said. "Follow the path to the creek and see if maybe she's there."

It didn't make sense that JZ would have used the tunnel to leave the fortress to simply go to the creek, especially alone.

"What do you think's going on, Sky?" King asked in quiet.

"I don't know," Sky said. "It doesn't make sense. Were the doors secure this morning on the walk-through, Leo?"

"The shutters and doors were secure," Leo said. "Ms. Betty was the only thing that was different from usual, but she was on the couch all night. The lady sleeps like she's dead."

"So, nobody got in," Sky said. "So she left, for whatever reason. Dammit, she knows better. Okay, listen. King and I will follow the path to the creek to see if we can find her. The rest of you, go back to the fortress and wait. Secure the door to the tunnel in the basement and stay inside until we get back."

"Just you two going in there?" Wyatt said.

"We'll radio for backup if we need it," Sky said. "We don't know what we may find, so I don't want the others along."

Sky went to turn around and Wyatt grabbed her arm. "We're going to find her," he said, his blue eyes piercing her own.

"Come on, King," she said.

The two pushed through the brush and headed toward the path to the clearing. Both held their guns at the ready, and although they were anxious to find JZ, they did not want to shout for her, and they did not want to proceed in haste. As they moved stealthily through the woods, they scanned, listened, and stopped every few feet to observe.

Nothing seemed miss to their eyes and ears. Birds sang, squirrels and rabbits scurried through the brush, branches swayed in the breeze, and little bugs hummed. It was only logical on such a beautiful day that they would find JZ sitting on a rock or at the creek bed, reflecting. They would scold her for being so selfish and stupid, but she would be safe, and they would all be relieved and go back to the fortress, where they'd eat breakfast together and tell more stories—maybe even one that had been read from Sim's journals.

Then they came upon the clearing. The vision of a happy ending evaporated as they came upon JZ's lifeless body, strung up on a tree trunk with rope, her arms splayed out on a cross bar made from a fallen limb. She was crucified, her body drenched in dry blood and her head hanging limply, facing the ground.

Sky dropped to her knees and cried out while King approached JZ slowly, in shock, not believing that it could really be her. JZ was beyond dead, her two axes laying primly at her feet. Whoever had done it, killed her viciously, and by the looks of it, intended to make her a spectacle for the rest of them. He observed the wound in her stomach and across her neck as he attempted to lift her head up to see if there were any signs of life. She had a note pinned to her body, which he read with a tilted head.

You will all march obliviously to your destruction.

He turned back to Sky, who had her face buried in her hands. He didn't know what to say to her. There was no way to assuage the pain of this moment, which would be etched in their minds for the rest of eternity. The deaths of the others in the battle with Zagan paled in comparison to this outrage; at least dying in defense of their home made some sort of sense, whereas this was senseless.

King backed away from the tree slowly, wanting to look away from JZ, but not able to. Once alongside Sky, he reached down and snatched up her radio. His lips and mouth were suddenly dry as he sucked at the morning air.

"Uh, Wyatt, please," he said. "You copy?"

What would Sim do? What would Sim think?

"What's up, good buddy?" Wyatt returned. "Did you find her?"

Yes, we found her. She's been murdered. She's crucified on a tree and barely recognizable because she's been flayed by a knife.

"We did," King said. "She's gone."

"What?" Wyatt asked.

"Wyatt...She's dead."

King took JZ's body down from the tree, and she fell limply onto his shoulder.

Sky uttered not a word. She collected JZ's bloodied axes, one in each hand, and followed King back to the fortress, JZ in tow.

She must have fought hard with her axes so bloody. Unless they used her own axes to kill her. Why, JZ? Why? How could you do such a thing?

She probably found out about you...your cowardice. You running away when you could have helped me.

It was her uncle Mike, memories of that last day with him intruding into her headspace again. Sky couldn't remember if her mind spoke the truth of that day, nor could she understand why, after all this time, those days were returning to her thoughts. Stress? She loved Uncle Mike, and he loved her. Even if she had left him vulnerable when she could have helped, he would not have blamed her. Still, she could not shed the thoughts of wronging, and the yearning to find out what happened to him after she fled.

She tried to process what set of circumstances had led to JZ leaving the house and being murdered in such a way, but nothing she came up with made any sense. They were doing everything right. Exactly the way Sim would have expected.

Clearly, JZ wasn't.

She could not find the words to express how she felt about finding JZ strung to the tree. The entire way home, she thought of what she would tell the others about this. How would they handle it? JZ was a rock. No nonsense. The girl who could land an axe between the enemy's eyes at fifty paces, but also do the hair and nails of her loved ones with a delicate touch. Misty's confidante, roommate, and best friend.

Sky suddenly felt inadequate.

What didn't you see?

What didn't you do?

This could have been prevented if you only knew what was going on with JZ.

Short of the fortress compound, she let out a loud scream. King turned around and placed JZ gently on the ground, as her dead weight on his shoulder was no longer bearable.

"How could I have been so oblivious?" she asked as King stood before her, his hands on his sides.

"Sky...JZ left—"

"No, King!" She cried. "She was tricked or threatened. She wouldn't have left, otherwise. This failure is ours. We missed something. Maybe something with those men from the other day. Something at the creek, maybe? She was taking a long time going to the bathroom when we were there. Did she see something? Hear something that she was exploring on her own? We thought everything was going fine, and our blindness caught up with us."

"Everything *was* going fine," King said. "There was a reason we've been comfortable. Now, it's time to *not* be comfortable."

"If that's true, King," Sky said, "can we handle it? Are we equipped? There are more lives at stake."

"Sim probably felt the same way after Flip died," King said. "Zagan challenged him in ways he had never expected, and he was honest with that. It was his first real challenge, and this is ours."

Sky looked at him for further rescue.

King stepped closer to Sky, who was forlorn. In each of her blood-stained hands, she was holding one of JZ's axes out in front of her. King took the axes from her and placed them in his waistband. He then grabbed her hands, one in each of his. "This is not our fault. We will find out who did this, and they will pay."

"King…I'm afraid," Sky said, a look of terror in her eyes.

King had never seen Sky lost like this.

"You don't have to be, Sky," King reassured. "*I'm* here. We have the heights. I'm as shocked and upset as you are, but we cannot return home defeated. The others will need us more than ever. Remember how you handled things when Flip was murdered? We have to rise and find out what is going on here and handle it."

The two embraced. Sky cried on King's shoulders as he held her. When her tears ran their course, she composed herself. King scooped JZ into his thick arms and carried her close to his chest the rest of the way. As they entered the fortress compound, the others were standing in a line at the opposite end of the open field between the outhouse and the well, as if they were a team preparing to play a game. Sky rubbed the tears from her cheeks and fixed her posture.

"This is gonna be hard," King said.

Sky radioed across the field. "Wyatt...do you copy?"

"I sure do, Sky," he said. "I'm sorry."

"I don't want the others to see her like this," she said. "We need to wash her first, at the well. Please take the others inside. Misty is welcome to meet us and tell her to bring the key to the well cover. We'll bury her this afternoon."

"Copy that," Wyatt said. "What happened out there?"

Sky looked at Wyatt across the field, unblinking. "I don't know."

Sky and King waited until the crowd at the other end dispersed. Misty returned with the key to the well cover as they arrived with JZ's body. King placed her gently on the ground, and Misty knelt beside her and took one of her hands into her own. She trembled and sobbed.

"It's not possible," she said. "It's not possible."

But it was, Sky felt. The reality of an untimely death was reflected in their way of life since the plague began, and there was no sign that this would change any time soon. Even with all the progress. Even with the precautions. Even with the support of many good people, there were still others out there waiting for their moment to complete what the plague had not.

Death. The ruin of souls. The fall of man. The earth did not get this one right. It should have taken everyone and everything all at once. Not in pieces. Not like this.

"What good has Sim's mission done for any of us?" Misty asked. "If we're to die like this anyway, in spite of our best efforts."

"We don't have to die like this," King said.

"But we will!" Misty said. "It's a certainty. Maybe not every one of us, but most of us, before we see any sliver of hope in this world. This community...the heights...we're not creating any kind of world order. All we're doing is hiding in a building and carrying guns to go swimming in the creek until the next lunatic finds us and kills us. JZ was better than this."

King looked to Sky, whose hair danced in the morning breeze. He was counting on her words but could see she had nothing to offer.

"Misty," King said. "It starts here. We won't change the world overnight, but one day, it'll be the lunatics running and hiding. Not us."

"Do you know how many people have died in history fighting for a new way of life, Misty?" Sky asked. "We may all die, but I will never believe our lives were lost in vain. We can't lose hope."

Misty buried her head into JZ's body, stiff and cold though it was. "What do we do?"

"We move forward," Sky said. "Find out what's going on. Find the people who did this. Eliminate them and carry on."

Misty closed her eyes and mumbled a prayer over JZ's body. She then looked to the sky. King removed JZ's axes from his waistband and placed them beside the body. Misty picked one up and eyed it curiously with a smile.

"I would have loved to have seen that fight," Misty said. "You know she at least got one of them."

"Probably two," Sky said.

The trio worked together to clean JZ's body. And when the task was completed, Misty went up to her room to retrieve JZ's collection of grooming tools: a brush, makeup, nail polish, and blush. She spent several minutes making her look as pretty in death as she had in life, because it was JZ who ordinarily tended to the orphans in this way.

With King's help, they straightened out her body as best they could, and placed it in the hole they dug in Usland, alongside all the others that had lost their lives. They then invited the others to bid their farewells before covering her body and sending it back to the earth.

There was little conversation in the group as the day wore on. Sky retreated to her room, and King, along with Wyatt, checked in with the others periodically throughout the day to provide counsel. That evening,

King broke out the Ramen to keep things simple at dinner, and because everyone loved it. Because now, even the smallest things went a long way.

It was clear Ms. Betty, whose trip to the heights was understandably delayed another day, was feeling awkward. She kept to the side and offered condolences but remained relatively quiet in the proceedings. King asked her if she would mind Yamil and Miracle during the day while Sky retreated, and Ms. Betty was delighted to fill in where needed as the rest of them processed the enormity of the situation. Yamil and Miracle were sad as well, but they were young and didn't quite understand that JZ would never return to them.

Sky did not report to dinner. She had sequestered herself to her room since JZ's burial, and though her grief was understandable, King worried how the impact of this tragedy would affect her long term.

They had lived in peace for so long since Zagan's fall and Sim's death. They did so much and believed to the core that their efforts had not only made changes that would lead to a new local order, but that they had already achieved it. Now, a new reality had emerged, and their resolve would be tested in a way it never had been. It would be the first time they'd understand what it was like for Sim when Zagan reared his demonic head in their lives.

One step forward, two steps backward.

King realized that even with JZ's death still raw, there was no time to hit the pause button. Even without Sky present at dinner, he needed to take time to speak on matters of all things pertinent to their mission and survival, lest everyone let their guard down and invite more terror and death into their community.

"As you guys can see," King began, "Sky is taking some time to herself. Like all of you, JZ's death has hit her hard. But in a different way. Things have been going well for the last several months, and it was easy to think that they would always go well. So, now, like Sim with Zagan, *we* are put to the test for the first time without him. The only question moving forward is, how are we going to handle it?"

Everyone had stopped eating except for Miracle, who was in the middle of slurping down a noodle. Yamil elbowed him in the side.

"The truth is...we're in danger again," King said. "Someone has attacked us, but in a much different way than Zagan. It could be a fluke...something JZ got herself involved in, or it could be something more. We just don't know. But now more than ever, we must remember everything Sim taught us. Because if we do, it will save us from anyone else being hurt."

Wyatt cleared his throat. "I'm still thinking about those guys from the other day," he said. "That visit still isn't sitting right with me. It's the only thing that's been off here lately. Just the way that guy, Vash, smiled at me. They weren't interested in the heights."

King was suddenly reminded of the probing attack Zagan launched to test their defenses before fully revealing his intentions.

Could that be why those men paid them a visit?

King turned to Ms. Betty, who was studiously eating her Ramen noodles as if to avoid becoming part of the discussion. "Were you across the street with your flashlight the night before you checked in here, Ms. Betty?"

The woman looked up, a noodle hanging from her mouth, which was surrounded by deep wrinkles. "Oh, yes, that was probably me. I can't see well in the dark. I didn't think it would be appropriate knocking on your door so late at night...so I waited."

King nodded. "Just keep doing what we're doing, everyone. And for God's sake, don't leave the house alone! How many people have to die before we realize that leaving the house alone could be a death sentence. The whole point of Sim bringing us here was to protect us within the walls of this place. He had rules that, to this day, we have to follow. At all times, dammit! Do you understand?"

Everyone acknowledged their understanding and agreement.

"Good. Our general patterns are sufficient. Just raise your awareness levels. If anything strikes you as something that is not normal, I don't care how small, get on a walkie and let us all know."

"What about my tooth?" Teddy said.

"We have to get you up there," King said, sinking back in his chair. "Ms. Betty, too. We don't have a choice. Sky and Wyatt will be fine with the others while we're away. We have to update Charlie, too, and bring more people back down with us to stay until we figure out what's going on. I'm worried this may only be the beginning of something worse."

"That's a good idea," Wyatt said. "I think, for the time being, extra sets of eyes will be a smart move."

King, sitting in Sky's chair at the head of the table, put in his final words. "We all loved JZ, but we know that this world is unforgiving. We know it is dangerous. We all love each other but understand that we can't lose ourselves in this type of tragedy. Like with Flip. We can be sad without getting lost. We must continue to be strong for ourselves and for the rest of us that are still here. Remember that."

Not much else was said around the dinner table about the road ahead as everyone finished their Ramen noodles, each steeped in his or her own thoughts.

King, more engrossed in worry than he let on, was thinking how hard it was to live in a world where there was no time to mourn. No time to remember. No time to catch a breath. How JZ had died that day, and yet the conversation could not revolve around this tragic loss, her memory, or her legacy. It had to focus on why she died and what they would have to do to make sure nobody else did.

Misty was thinking about how they were in a constant state of battle where nobody ever won, lost, or went home at the end. How they could never sigh in relief and exclaim that they had made it, because they were never home free. How their lives were a perpetual state of anticipation, like being caught in the funnel of a tornado that spun round and round without ever stopping.

And the rest of them, though saddened without JZ, were thinking about the salty taste of Ramen on their tongues, about chess, or about what fun they had swimming the day before... The simpler things that distracted them from a life lived under constant threat.

Wyatt, though, was only thinking about how they were the pioneers of a new world, and in being such, they might never be saved. But their true purpose might be to lay the groundwork for others to be saved instead.

Salvation for themselves might only mean salvation for others.

Nine

LATER IN THE DAY, while Ms. Betty was minding Yamil and Miracle in the playroom, she called them over to her. It was the moment she had been waiting for, as Leo had not let her out of his sight, per the fortress protocol for visitors. When she wasn't on the couch, he was on her tail watching her every move.

The boys, always eager for attention, dropped their toy blocks and flocked to her side. They sat beside her and waited.

"Aren't you sweethearts," she said. "And I have a special surprise for you."

The boys looked at each other with excited smiles.

"You must be missing this man, Sim, who used to take care of you." she said.

Yamil and Miracle both nodded.

"What if I told you a secret?" Ms. Betty said. "But if I do, you can't tell another soul."

Yamil and Miracle exchanged looks. Miracle nodded first, and Yamil reluctantly followed suit.

"Well," Ms. Betty said. "I actually came here not because I wanted to go to the heights, but because I wanted to bring you to a place where you can see Sim. He's alive and waiting for you."

"What you mean?" Yamil asked.

"I mean," Ms. Betty said, "he's not really dead, you see. His spirit...his energy...it lives. Do you know what a revenant is?"

Yamil and Miracle shook their heads.

"It's simply a spirit who comes back from the dead," she said. "Sim, he's here, and I can arrange it so you can see him."

"How?" Yamil asked.

"Tomorrow, you'll see," Ms. Betty continued. "After I give you the word, you go out to the outer edge of the property in the back, and there will be a friend of mine, waiting. He will escort you to where Sim is. And won't that be amazing?"

Yamil scrunched up his tiny face. "We're not supposed to leave the fortress alone. King and Sky said. It's a big rule."

"Ahhh," Ms. Betty said. "But you won't be leaving alone. You'll be with Miracle, and the two of you will be quite the heroes when you bring Sim back to everyone, now won't you?"

Yamil and Miracle both smiled. Miracle clasped his hands together. "He'll come back?"

"Yes," Ms. Betty said, her blue eyes intensifying. "Can you imagine such a thing? And it's the perfect time to have him return. He's so needed now. That's why I am going to offer this to you."

"Tomorrow?" Yamil confirmed.

"By the cemetery," Ms. Betty said. "I will let you know when. Don't forget. And don't tell a soul, or it won't work."

"Fine," Yamil said.

"I can't wait," Miracle said.

The boys went back to play while Ms. Betty watched them intently.

Like taking candy from a baby.

Moments later, Leo entered the playroom.

"There you are," he said. "You're supposed to be with me at all times."

"Oh, sorry, dear," Ms. Betty said. "One of your friends asked me to watch the boys, given everything that was going on. It's such a tragedy."

"Yes, it's really sad," Leo said. "You're not here at the best time, I guess, but we'll get you to the heights tomorrow, first thing."

Ms. Betty flashed Leo a smile, hiding her sinister heart beneath it.

If Vash and his church members were going to fulfill their devious plan, they needed more help.

While he, Balaam, and Amon stayed close to the fortress on recon duty, Pan returned to their current stomping ground, a former group home on the twisty Redemption Road, where they had been gathering as a church for the past twenty years. Only a handful of members survived the virus, including he, Zagan, Vash, Amon, and Balaam, and they knew right where to go to find each other amidst the mayhem the virus had caused.

When things settled, and most people had fallen, they journeyed on a mission to the headquarters of the Church of Satan to see if other members had survived and to lie in wait for their brethren. It's where they met Mantus, who had more recently fallen to JZ's axe. Of course, Zagan had fallen before that time, and it disheartened those who remained, because he was an influential member of the church ever since being inducted by Vash years before. He was also one of Vash's closest friends.

At the time of his departure from the group in Massachusetts, the other members begged Zagan to wait, but he insisted he return home in advance of the group to see if anyone else might be waiting at their location on Redemption Road. He was anxious to build back their membership and become strong again. But as he got closer to home, he started to hear more about the fortress, and those stories piqued his interest.

The rest was history.

Pan caught up with Ms. Betty at the home. She did her best to make the two-story structure a livable environment for their group, but it was all in vain. The former group home had been closed ten years before the fall. It was structurally unsound: windows had been boarded up, interior walls were collapsing, the floors were littered with wood and glass, kitchen cabinets were warped and decrepit, the hardwood floors rotted, stairways collapsing, and furniture had long since been removed.

Ms. Betty still kept things as tidy as possible with the promise that they would soon re-establish themselves somewhere new. Currently, their sleeping arrangements consisted of old mattresses, blankets, and pillows. They had no arsenal or consistent food supply. They lived off the land and ate as needed in order to survive. They captured prey and cooked it over fire, and they obtained water from a nearby stream.

They could have done this anywhere, but the location on Redemption Road was part of their sacred history. Over the years, they had gathered with their church and indulged in rituals and prayers, many times over a roaring bonfire in the backyard. They were devoted to what they considered sacred ground and would not consider leaving until they found the perfect spot to rebuild their church.

When Pan entered the main entrance, he saw Ms. Betty lighting the lantern on the reception area desk.

"Did you find what you were looking for?" she asked.

"We did," Pan said. "We discovered Zagan's resting place. The grounds are sacred, and the building lavish. Vash has deemed it the perfect site for our relocation. But before we can secure this place, we need your help."

"How so?" she asked.

"The occupants of this place operate with strict protocol, and we can exploit that by sending you in as an interested party."

"Interested in what?" she asked.

"Finding a home," Pan said. "They won't let you stay long term, but they will let you stay long enough to be escorted somewhere else. During that time, you can gather information on how many people are living there, and maybe even make one or more of them disappear."

"Disappear?" she said.

Pan smiled. "They are children. Children trust caring adults. This is something you could use to your advantage while there."

"I don't like children," Ms. Betty said, her face hardened.

"This isn't about children," Pan reminded. "This is about our future and our plans."

"I can certainly pretend well enough to do what needs to be done," she smiled.

"That's all we ask," Pan said. "Leave with me now, then, and we will have you in place by morning."

The two left that evening and made it back to the others near the fortress later that night. They devised a generally wicked plan that they hoped would strike at the hearts of the orphans' happy home. After which, they may not have to do a thing but watch the orphans' world collapse.

The next morning, Ms. Betty was ready to do her part for the glory of her church.

Sky emerged from her room after everyone had gone to sleep, save Leo, who was on the first shift of the overnight watch. He was in the living room peering out the window, eyes wide, rifle in hand, Gigi lying on the floor beside the couch where Ms. Betty had taken up for another night. His face was aglow, courtesy of a soft battery-powered light that was affixed to the wall above the couch. It had a button to turn it on and off. Leo did not like being in total dark. The darkness of the new world was much different than that of old.

Leo would get up every fifteen minutes and circulate through the first floor of the house with Gigi scampering behind to make sure that not a creature was stirring before lying back down. He would repeat this process over the course of his two-hour shift.

Baby would pass her time sitting on the main stairwell staring at the front door, as if mentally opposing anyone who would dare try to break in, and remembering the days when she and Big Will were charged with opening the front doors on command.

Misty would never sit down during her shift. She would walk in circles on the first floor of the house to keep awake. Or maybe she was nervous and had learned from Sim that an active pace helped to calm.

King would traverse the entire house on a loop to make sure he had an eye on everything. He would complain that the first floor was hard to see, because they had to keep the windows blocked at night with interior shutters made of wood due to their proximity to ground level, whereas the upper-level windows could be left as is.

One could look upon the city through the windows on those upper floors and not feel trapped. Even at night, there were universal lights to be in awe of, even after the artificial lights of humankind shut off. Though the darkness prevailed, the stars and moon offered a glimpse of the world beyond the walls of the fortress at a time when one might wonder if the world had been swallowed up whole.

Sky made eye contact with Leo, and Gigi raised her head as she entered the living room. The two acknowledged each other silently while Ms. Betty slept. She made rounds to each bedroom, stopping at the thresholds of their doors to watch the orphans sleep. It reminded her of simpler times, when her only job was to take care of the little ones and make sure their needs were met. Filling Sim's shoes was not anything she was prepared for, and it gave her some insight into the pressure Sim must have felt trying to keep the fortress vital and the orphans safe.

She grabbed an apple from the kitchen table. She was hungry from having skipped dinner, but she wasn't a huge fan of Ramen anyway, and she needed time to collect herself after JZ's murder.

She used the kitchen stairs to ascend to the second floor. She stepped into Yamil and Miracle's room and thought of Sim's journal entries...hundreds of them: days-gone-by stories, perhaps never told. She looked forward to reading through his writings and learn more about him. The boys were curled up together in a single bed, though there were two beds in the room. They often slept together. They had formed a connection over the years almost like that of twins; one never went anywhere without the other. She wondered how healthy it was for their co-dependency to continue as they got older, and Leo, at least, was yearning for them to shed their innocent skin and become part of the new world. But Sky was the one holding them back. She loved their sweetness. She loved that they were just children, even in this world, not yet contaminated by the realities of existing in such a place. Sim saw this in them too and allowed it. The babies of the family. Spare the rod. Maybe Sim believed that because the boys were so little, that the rest of them in the house could make enough difference so that they would not have to become what everyone else had: Hardened. Cynical. Paranoid. Trapped. Maybe Sim wanted Yamil and Miracle to be real children.

She moved to King's room next, where Wyatt also took up residence. The door was closed, and intruding on the men seemed inappropriate, and knocking so late at night equally so. She placed her forehead on his door while she thought of King and how much he had changed since Sim's death to try and step up and help fill the void.

She moved next to Misty and JZ's room. The door was open. She noticed Misty was sleeping in JZ's bed, clutching JZ's favorite plush pillow. It was pink and made of silk. JZ had found it on a run, and it had become like a security blanket for her.

She listened to Misty's soft breathing and tried to imagine how she was feeling. Sim had tried to prepare them for the reality of death and to teach them that they should not be afraid of loving someone, but to understand that love comes at a cost, more often in this world than the old.

The moonlight poured through the window, immersing Misty in light. Sky skirted around the bed and stood at the window. As she glanced to the road in the front of the house, she saw a man standing in the moonlight, hands in his pockets and staring at the fortress. It was hard to see anything but his face, and though he was at a distance, she knew he was staring up at her.

Sky felt her flesh tingle and her heart race as she stared at this man who contested her with a willful look of his own that cut through the night sky between them.

Just run. I'll lead them away. Just run. I'll lead them away.

She heard her uncle Mike again in her mind. To what end, she wasn't sure, but she suddenly wished he was there to protect her like he had done that day. Or Sim. Someone. This was the man who likely murdered JZ, and she had no understanding of why, or what he might do next. Whoever he and his men were, they were stalking them for a reason. That much was clear to her now.

"What are you looking at?" Misty asked, shaking Sky from her trance.

Sky snapped a glance at Misty. "He's there."

She bolted from the room. Misty jumped out of bed after grabbing a pistol from the nightstand and followed Sky down the front stairs.

"Leo, Gigi!" Sky cried as she thrust open the fortress doors and ran down the steps into the street.

Leo and Misty followed behind, yet they were not sure of why they were in the middle of the road at night, unprotected.

Sky stood in the center of the street, staring in the direction of where she had seen the man from the window. Gigi ran to her side and barked ferociously in the direction that Sky was staring.

"I'm here!" she screamed. Her voice echoed. "What are you waiting for?"

Leo and Misty turned in all directions, guns raised, confused, and trying to find a target. Gigi continued to bark wildly.

"Come and get us, you coward!" Sky screamed.

"I don't see anything," Leo said, panic in his voice.

"We're not safe out here, Sky!" Misty warned. "This could be what these people want. It might be exactly how they goaded JZ to leave."

It was the author Tolstoy who said the two most powerful warriors are patience and time.

Sky heard Sim's voice and remembered the day of the probing attack by Zagan, when his men tried to stir them up by throwing things at the fortress. They all wanted to go out and confront them, but Sim wouldn't allow it. Yet here she was.

Wyatt and King, disturbed from their sleep, rushed out the front door as well.

"What in tarnation is going on out here?" Wyatt asked.

"There's nothing out here," King said. "We need to get in."

Sky turned to him. "He was here." She pointed a short distance up the hill where a white rusted out car with flat tires was parked along the curb.

"Whoever these people are, they are just playing games with us, Sky," King said.

She reached up and grabbed King by the collar. "Are you calling JZ's death a game?" she hissed.

"You damn well know that's not what I'm saying," King said.

Wyatt stepped toward the two. "Let's just all go inside and we'll—"

"I'm telling you he was standing here. One of those men from the other day. We need to go after him and chase him down and kill him while we can."

"It's the middle of the night," King said. "We're not going to catch anything out there but death. Don't you see? We don't even know who they are or how many of them there are. The only thing we're certain of is that they might want us all dead. Like Zagan did. And if that is the case, we can't make it that easy for them."

"I told you I saw flashlights the other night," Teddy said, standing in the doorway rubbing his eyes.

"Go check on Ms. Betty," King said.

Teddy returned inside and found Ms. Betty standing at the front window in the living room. She had opened the shutters and was watching the scene on the street.

Sky turned to Leo. "Did you not see him out here?" she asked, frustration in her voice.

"I don't have my eyes out the window every second," Leo said. "If you think we should be stationed at the window all night, then we'll need to start putting two guards up instead of one."

Sky ignored him and looked up at the roof and saw Skinny Jim standing at the top, staring down upon them. She radioed up to him.

"Jim," she said. "You saw nothing out here?"

"Nothing but the moon," he said. "But I was on the lower roof before all of the commotion."

She pressed the radio to her mouth. "You're always on the lower roof! It's time to start spending your time on the upper roof where you can see the entire perimeter! That's twice you missed what's going on in the front because you're in the back!"

"Sorry, Sky," Skinny Jim said. "Still getting a feel for this gig. What's going on down there, anyway?"

Sky shook her head. "Just scan the area with the night vision again and make sure we're clear."

"Roger that," Skinny Jim said.

"Let's get in, Sky," King said. "If that guy wants to stand around out here at night and stare at us, then let him. At some point, he'll catch a bullet in the ass, but what's not going to happen is him getting at us if we stay inside. Nighttime is no time to be picking a fight."

"No doubt, Sky," Wyatt said. "JZ's death is unimaginable, but it won't be in vain. We have a lot of experience with how to handle threats. So, let's keep our cool for now."

The gang went inside and closed the doors behind them.

"My goodness," Ms. Betty said. "I've never seen so much drama. Are you sure you guys can't use an extra hand around here for a little while? You've surely got your own hands full."

"It might not be a bad idea, Sky," Wyatt said. "With some of us leaving to the heights tomorrow, it may be convenient to have an extra hand."

"We're going to be bringing down more people from the heights anyway when we come back," King said.

"Misty?" Sky said. "What do you think?"

"Fine with me," she said.

Sky turned to Ms. Betty. "It looks like you'll be here for a while. But it's no picnic, as you can see."

"I'll be fine, dear," Ms. Betty said.

Leo swapped guard shifts with Misty, and everyone else returned to their rooms.

Sky pulled out one of Sim's journals and breezed through it, looking for something that might help her cope. She stopped at an entry about Flip.

Day 1006,

The worst has happened again. I vowed after Elizabeth's death that I would remain level-headed and subscribe to a level of emotional detachment with regards to the fate of these orphans. With death so close all the time, it's only sensible. Even in the midst of feeling love for others, I cannot let my emotions defeat me as they nearly did in the weeks that followed the taking of my wife and daughter's lives. People are going to die. Maybe some or all of these children. Maybe me. It doesn't mean I didn't care or didn't try.

I ran out to avenge Flip's death, and when I returned, I felt silly. The others looked to me to lead, and yet I allowed myself to be led, by someone who should never have an ounce of control over me. We have to be sensible and not be reactive. To allow others to have control over us makes us their puppets. We need to be the masters of our own fate.

Death is only one part of life. It's sad, but like with any other emotion, we need to allow sadness and grief to pass, and pass quickly, so we can live in the moment and not in the past. It's hard, yes, but it's a necessity, I've learned. This world and every moment that passes in front of us is a gift to behold, and we must cherish it by accepting the reality around us, not as defined by the past or what we might worry about in the future.

I loved you Flip, but you are gone now. We will see you again. But for now, there are other moments to live for.

Sky, tired, closed the journal and thought about the parallels between Sim's entry and her own reaction that night. He was right about how he reacted to Flip's death. She had acted hastily too, and she remembered something he had told her after one of her arguments with him that also seemed relevant:

Nobody respects a leader who lacks self-control.

She had to do better.

Though she wanted to sleep, she felt compelled to visit the library and retrieve a notebook of her own. If Sim found peace and reflection by writing down his thoughts and experiences, why could she not do the same?

She turned on a light and found a marble notebook, of which there were many, and opened it up to the first page. She smiled, feeling as if she were in Language Arts class at school. Since those normal days, she was the one that had to teach everyone else—and on top of it, herself—though in his day, Sim taught her a great many things.

He taught her more advanced math, and they would pick up copies of the same books, reading them together and holding book clubs at night. They would sometimes fight about the stories, their morals, characters, and meanings, but that was the point. She always felt it was their way of connecting on a more personal level, and Sim did that quite well with the others.

King wasn't a big reader, but he played chess, and he and Sim would share that. Sim would build structures with Leo, let JZ do his hair, and he would ask Misty to share her stories, even though he might have tired of hearing them all the time. Teddy only wanted to use him as a jungle gym, and Sim happily served that purpose with all the boys. Sim was special in more ways than just being their protector. And maybe nobody realized it, but one day they would, looking back. Like Sky was now.

Sim couldn't not be who he was. And even if he was pretending to himself that building the fortress was an obligation for his absolution, everyone else knew better.

Dear Journal,

I don't even know what day it is. Does it matter? We lost JZ today. It was horrifying. We were hoping to never lose any more of us, and maybe we tricked ourselves into believing that if we did everything the way Sim taught, nobody would ever die. But Sim never told us we wouldn't die. In fact, he always put it in our heads that we might. So, why would we be surprised if one of us did?

My mother once told me that we don't mourn for those who die, we mourn for ourselves. Sim came to believe that we should let sorrow and grief pass quickly, so we could get on with facing the present reality. Oddly, I still want to be amazed by the world. By the moment. Sometimes, I just don't know how.

I think about Sim all the time, as well as my parents and my Uncle Mike, whose fate I cannot be sure of. He calls to me still, and I hear his voice all the time. I don't how to let go of it all. Practice, maybe.

Tomorrow will be a new day. We will enjoy the sunlight or rain, whatever comes. King will take Teddy with Misty to the heights, and the rest of us will remain, yet all of us will remain true to what we learned and what we believe.

We will remember JZ fondly forever and visit her in Usland, and we will not let her death haunt us. She was beautiful, carefree, and her very presence ignited a room.

That's all that matters now.

When Sky concluded her journal, she did one final check of all the rooms. The rest of the night was quiet, and the entire night might have been so, had she read Sim's journal earlier in the evening and taken heed to ignore the taunting of these men from outside their walls. Still, she wondered what their endgame was, and worried for the day she would find out.

Tomorrow would be a new day to practice how to live and lead, and Sky was anticipating the challenge.

Ten

Vash, followed by Amon and Balaam, entered their rundown residence at Valley Hall, four miles east of the fortress. Pan remained near the fortress to keep an eye on things while Ms. Betty was setting up a devious plan from within it that would ultimately involve him.

The trio of men entered through the main doors, which had fallen to rot long before the fall. Vash snatched up one of the burning lamps, which was welcoming them with flickering light on the decrepit desk that used to be the group home's reception area. They followed the hallway, which was littered with debris and hanging wires, past a bathroom, around a corner, past a set of former dormitories, and out the side door that led to the back.

Balaam's arm was in a sling from JZ's assault. Vash had cleaned and stitched up his wound the night of their return. He had bandaged the side of his own head with gauze and buried the pain of having lost half his ear. He could only wait until what he had left healed and scarred before letting it breathe again.

For now, it was time to move forward and ritualize their success in appreciation of their accomplishments. It was the first of many great rituals, rites, and celebrations to come, so they believed.

The men stood, bathed in the light of the full moon, which hovered over the vacant lot of overgrown green space, dotted with rotted picnic tables and a weed-ridden former flower garden. They stood around a cleared spot in the middle of the yard where the ground was stained black from previous fires before moving to the outskirts of the property to collect wood and kindling for a new one.

Vash prepared the collection of wood and carefully formed a tent with it that was taller than him, which he then ignited using brush and leaves that easily caught with the help of the kerosene lamp. Within minutes, a fire roared, and the men were in awe of it as smoke and ash eclipsed the bright light.

Amon retrieved a picture from his pants pocket and unfolded it. It was a crude drawing composed of four individual pictures, each one in a separate quadrant of the larger page. The first was a depiction of JZ talking with Mantus in the woods. The second was of her being surrounded by Vash and the others. The third was a crude depiction of Vash sinking a sword into her stomach, and the fourth was a picture of JZ crucified on a tree.

Amon tossed it into the fire, and the fire devoured it quickly and anxiously as the men raised their arms and chanted together as one.

Moon. Moon. We call upon you.

Accept our sacrifice and await more soon.

Her time has come, and theirs will too.

Moon. Moon. We call upon you.

Let them cry and meet their demise,

So that Zagan will rise.

Moon. Moon. We call upon you.

They repeated the chant over and over, after which they stood by the fire and watched it burn.

At one point, Amon said, "I'm glad we all found each other again after the fall, Vash."

Vash stared into the fire, feeling the warmth of it on his face. "There were dozens of you over the years that I taught and freed, Zagan among them. There may be more that lived through this disease, and who will return. We will all unite, and as we grow our membership again, we will create a new order. One like this world has never seen."

"Zagan shall be redeemed," Balaam said. "And reborn."

"He shall," Vash said.

"What next?" asked Balaam.

"Patience," Vash said. "While Ms. Betty's wheels turn, we will await her intel. With the slaughter of one of their own, they will step up their measures and look to kill quick, as they expect us at every corner. Let them continue to look for us while we keep an eye on them. When they least expect it, we will strike again, and we shall not stop until the last of them are gone."

As the fire burned, the men retired to their dorms for rest, for their work was far from done.

Before dawn, and a couple of hours after the midnight mayhem caused by Pan revealing himself to the fortress, Ms. Betty woke and rose from the couch. Misty, her eyes fixed outside the window, noticed right away and acknowledged her.

"Can't sleep?" Misty asked.

"Could you blame me?" she said. "Things have been a bit tense around here."

"It's not usually like this," Misty said. "Normally, things are calm. Now, one more of us is dead and just like that...everything changes in the blink of an eye."

"I'm sorry for your loss, dear," Ms. Betty said. "But we die in this world."

"I've learned that, like many, the hard way," Misty said, still looking out the window.

"I would like to go to my shopping cart for a book, if I could," Ms. Betty said. "I'm a bit restless and returning to my story could help tire my eyes."

"It's dangerous out there alone," Misty said. "And we're supposed to stay with you. I will go out with you and offer cover while you retrieve your book."

Ms. Betty rose from the couch, and Misty opened the door for her. The two proceeded down the fortress steps and to the side of the brick building where Ms. Betty's shopping cart was stowed. Misty shone her flashlight into the cart to help Ms. Betty find her book.

"There it is," she said, snatching up the book as she left a small note behind, stuck in between some of the canned goods.

She had composed the note from scrap paper and a pencil she had found in the kitchen during the rare moments she found to a steal away from the orphans' glances while on the couch. They typically ignored her when she was sedentary.

The two walked back inside, and Ms. Betty returned to the couch, book in hand. She turned on a soft light and continued where she had left off, satisfied that her job had been done.

Meanwhile, Pan, who had taken up a spot behind a house across the street, waited for the two to go back inside before pulling out his own night vision goggles and placing them over his eyes. He scanned the roof of the fortress and noticed the roof guard, though standing tall, was turned away. He spied inside each front window but did not see anyone.

Earlier in the night, he tested them by letting his presence be known to see what their response would be. He expected they might shoot from their windows. But instead, they paraded out front. This amused him.

On their way down from Valley Hall, he and Ms. Betty discussed how they would exchange intelligence if she were admitted, and the agreement was via notes left in her shopping cart, a prop deliberately brought into the proceedings. So, when he saw her come out in the middle of the night, he knew she had something to share.

Not seeing anyone through his night vision goggles, he dashed across the street to the fortress's right side. He viewed the contents of the cart through his night spectacles and saw the note she had left behind. He sat with his back against the fortress wall as he unrolled the small piece of scrap paper.

Staying to sink teeth in deeper. Watch rear property tomorrow a.m. for two boys who will be coming out for you to "lead them to Sim." Take them to VH. Wait our return. 10 total. 3 on the road tomorrow. 2 will be in your care. 5 will be left. Must act before they bring more.

Pan ripped up the letter and let the breeze take it as he tossed his head back against the cold brick. He smiled, and when the time was right, he moved into the wooded lot, up the hill, and brought himself back around to the rear of the fortress, where he hid behind a portion of the incomplete perimeter wall.

There he would wait for his arrivals. Bring them to Sim, he would.

Eleven

*W*E, THE ORPHANS OF *the new world, pledge to: do our best, work together, defend our home, live and die for one another, love, lead, remember. We are the fortress, and the fortress is us.*

As they wrapped up saying the pledge, there was silence at the table. Breakfast was over, and it was time for Teddy, King, and Misty to leave on their journey to the heights. JZ's death was still raw, and it was a difficult time for them to be apart. But Teddy's health was a priority, as was bringing more people back from the heights to help them prevail against this new threat.

"Before you leave," Sky began. "I found another entry in Sim's journal that I thought might inspire us all while we are apart."

"His journals bring back so many memories," Misty said. "Let's hear it."

Day 1007

This journey to the heights is different. We lost Flip and we need help. This is what I should have waited for. I should not have chased after Zagan in a rage. I could have been killed. King could have been killed. And for what?

We don't need to be afraid. We are the future, and if Zagan wasn't afraid himself, he would not be pursuing us. When others out there seek to bring us harm, it is only because we are a threat. In this world, love is a threat.

But we are not alone. They are alone. We have each other, and all the people of the heights along with us. We are an army. An army of God bringing light back to this world. So we will travel, and bring back with us the flame that will shine bright for the world to see.

Let us celebrate Flip's life, and our own, for we are the fortress, and always will be.

"Oh, Sim," Baby said, clasping her hands together. "He knows just what to say."

"He sounds very special," Ms. Betty said, leaning forward over the table.

Wyatt cleared his throat. "I have something I wanted to show you too...Kind of a lesson, you might say."

Just then, Wyatt pulled a bunch of unsharpened pencils from his back pocket.

He passed a single pencil to Leo. "Go ahead and see if you can break the pencil, Leo."

Leo smiled, his tongue out. He took the pencil and snapped it in half. "A cinch!"

"I want to break a pencil," Teddy whined.

"Go for it," Wyatt said. He handed one to Teddy and he snapped it in half.

"Yeah, that was cool," Teddy said. "Let me do it again."

"Now, calm down, Teddy," Wyatt said. "I won't have enough if you break them all, but as long as you got your motor revving, take the rest of these pencils together and see if you can break them all at once."

Teddy grabbed the nine remaining pencils and clustered them together. He then took both hands and tried to break all the pencils in half at once. His face turned red as he grunted. Eventually, he gave up.

"Hey," he said. "You tricked me."

"It's not a trick," Wyatt said. "Go ahead, Leo, you try."

He handed the pencils over to Leo, and Leo went through the same motions as Teddy, to no avail.

"You see!" Wyatt said.

"See what?" Baby asked.

Wyatt suddenly got all serious. "Alone, we break easy. Together, you can't break us."

"Sim couldn't have said it better than that, Wyatt," Sky said.

"You sure are a special lot," Ms. Betty said.

"Hot damn!" Skinny Jim yelled. "This place gets me right here." He pointed to his heart.

"I'm sure it does, Jim," Sky said. "Now go up and replace King, so they can depart." She turned to Teddy. "And good luck to you, Teddy. When you return, you'll be able to sleep better, we should hope."

"Not until my mother leaves me alone at night," Teddy said.

I am out here, Sky. Come look for me. I miss you.

Why, you, Uncle Mike? I don't think about my parents half as much as you.

Because you know I'm still alive. You feel it.

Sky considered these thoughts as she rose from the table.

"Not so fast, Yamil and Miracle," she said as they were about to scurry away like squirrels. "You have to clear the table and do the dishes."

Yamil and Miracle looked at each other then back to Ms. Betty.

"I'll help you boys so you can get on with your day," Ms. Betty winked.

"Leo, that means you'll be in the kitchen with Ms. Betty," Sky said.

"The one time you make these two do dishes and I still have to be in the kitchen anyway," Leo said. "She's a harmless old lady. Do I really have to babysit her still?"

Sky gave him a look of death, and Leo shied away quickly from her glower.

King barreled down the stairs and met Misty and Teddy at the front door.

"Stay vigilant," King said. "We'll be back before you know it, and with reinforcements. We're gonna find these people, and it'll be hell to pay."

"I hope you're right, King," Sky said.

With that, King, Misty, and Teddy left the fortress for the heights.

They climbed to the top of the hill through the woods alongside the fortress and made their way to the heights. The three kept a sharp eye on their surroundings to make sure they weren't being followed by these new threats that had so callously taken JZ's life.

"Why do you think they did this?" Misty asked, hugging an M-16 to her chest.

"We don't know," King said. "I'd like to think we may never know, but I don't think it was random. I think this is the beginning of something. I don't want to be scared about it, but I still wish I knew what was happening. We got to get this done fast and get back. It's like them pencils at breakfast. Our strength now has to be our numbers while we wait for their next move. Maybe we can send you back ahead of us with the extras."

"Smart thinking," Misty said. "Sky only wanted me to come for added security on the walk anyway."

"Is this going to hurt?" Teddy asked as they passed a golden field, the only sound the scuffing of their shoes on the cracked pavement.

"No more than the bullet you took in battle," King said.

"Yeah, yeah," Teddy said. "That's true. It can't hurt more than that. That was awful."

"It'll be fine, Teddy," King reassured.

"Well, at least I get to see the heights," he said. "I never get to go."

"You were there before," Misty said.

"Not a lot, and only once since Sim died," Teddy said.

"What's the big deal, anyway?" King said.

"It's just funner there," Teddy said. "All we get to do at the fortress is work."

They walked the road to the heights, stopping only when intercepted by a man named Scooter, who was about King's age, sporting a backward baseball cap. They recognized each other from King's stay after confronting Zagan, and they greeted each other with a special handshake and a hug.

"Hey, King," Scooter said revealing a smile with one missing tooth. "My main homey. How's it hanging, man?"

"We've seen better days," said King. "I have to fill Charlie in, but first we need to get this little man to Mrs. Chandler. He needs a tooth out."

King grabbed Teddy's shoulder and shook him gently.

"Ouch!" Scooter said. "No sweat. Teeth are the biggest pain in the ass in the apocalypse, man. The best bet is to just take them all out and go toothless, because they all gonna rot out anyway. Sure, you won't be able to eat meat as easily, but at least you won't have to deal with them."

"Yuck," Teddy said. "I brush every day. My teeth won't fall out."

"Every day, huh?" Scooter said. "Shit, King, that's got to be a lot getting all those little shits you live with to brush their teeth. That's a commitment, man."

"It's what we do," King said. "Plus, we don't eat all the nasty shit you do. It's that sugar that does it."

"Oh, man, well there's two things I need most in my life right now, King. That's sugar and *sugah*."

"Uh, hello," Misty finally chimed in.

Scooter turned as if seeing her for the first time. "Oh, yeah, sorry. What's your name again, little girl?"

"I'm not a little girl, and the name is Misty," she said. "I'm on a committee, you know, which is more than I can probably say for you."

"You into the politics and shit," Scooter said. "Dayum. Fancy committees and everything."

Misty rolled her eyes.

"Anyway, how's that dipshit, Skinny Jim? He must be driving you up a wall with all his 'Skinny Jim' this and 'Skinny Jim' that. Something not right with that boy."

"Thankfully, he stays on the roof most of the time," King said. "Not that he ever sees anything he's supposed to, but he's better than nothing."

Scooter burst out laughing until a voice scolded him from across the lawn.

"Scooter, get your ass over here now and stop with all the chitchat," a voice cried from a distance.

"Oh, shit," Scooter said. "That's Malayah. She thinks she runs the place now."

King saw Malayah approaching. She was the tallest woman he had ever seen. Easily six feet, with long blond hair and a taut body that looked like a physique belonging more to Hercules than to a woman.

"That's the queen of the herb?" King asked as she was approaching.

"Dayuum," Scooter said. "Don't call her that to her face."

When Malayah arrived beside them, Teddy glanced upward. He had to shield his eyes from the sun that silhouetted her.

"Whoa," he said. "You're tall."

"And you're short," she said in reply. "So, what's going on here? Do I know you guys?" she asked.

King cleared his throat. "I'm King, this is Teddy—"

"And I'm Misty," Misty said.

"We're from the fortress. We're here to see Charlie and Mrs. Chandler."

"Oh, right," Malayah said. "Now I remember you guys." She sized Misty up and then returned to King. "Well, *you*, anyway. You were the one that ran away from home, and then we had that big battle here and your caretaker he—"

"Yeah, we were there," Misty said.

"Excuse me," Malayah. "I'm just trying to put all these pieces together."

"Another time," King said. "It's important we see Charlie, and Teddy has an infected tooth."

"What do you need to see Charlie for?" Malayah asked. "I keep trying to warn him that his right-hand man, Tony, has something cooking, but he doesn't want to listen. I see the way that guy looks at him. He's up to no good. We're trying to get Charlie to let myself and Frankie take over security detail before he causes a mutiny."

"Doesn't a mutiny happen on a ship?" Misty questioned.

"Well, I don't know what they call it on land, but that's what's up," Malayah said.

Scooter laughed, and Malayah slapped him upside the head. "What are you laughing at, toothless? Had you brushed those damn teeth and gave one hoot about your human dignity you wouldn't be standing here looking like a six-year-old man-child right now."

"Um," King said. "We really have to get going."

She turned around and headed off. "Follow me and I'll get you over to Charlie's. I think my girl, Frankie, is over there now."

Scooter locked eyes with King and shrugged his shoulders. Malayah led them to Charlie's apartment, which was the same one he had confronted Zagan in. King was relieved to see that Charlie was sober as they entered to him on his feet arguing with a feisty Spanish woman. She was small in stature, with angular features, dressed in a set of camouflage pants and T-shirt. She had a crew cut and a fierce, hardened face.

"Frankie, baby!" Malayah yelled.

"What's up, mama," Frankie said. "Just trying to wake up Charlie a little bit with this whole Tony situation we've been talking about."

"Wow," Charlie said. "We have a whole gang. A quorum, in fact."

Frankie immediately interjected. "What about Tony?"

"We can discuss it later," Charlie said.

"We really should, Charlie," Malayah added. "We both saw him with a group of men, and they were all whispering and shit until we got close. Then they all got quiet real quick."

"True that, *pendejo*," Frankie affirmed. "Them fools are dirty. I don't trust them with all them guns, that's for sure."

"I said later, ladies," Charlie repeated, opening the door for them.

The two left the apartment while they continued to ramble back and forth with each other.

"I'll check you later, man," Scooter said.

Charlie closed the door behind them.

"JZ is dead," Teddy blurted out as Charlie came to face them.

Charlie's face turned a shade of white. "Dead?"

"Those men we were talking about at the meeting," Misty said. "We've seen them poking around, and yesterday when we woke up, JZ was gone. She had let herself out. And when we went to look for her, we found her in the woods..."

Misty looked at Teddy, whose eyes were wide. He hadn't seen her body. She wanted to spare him the details.

Charlie rubbed his chin. "Well, this doesn't make any sense. You said they were only standing there not really posing a threat that day. Just looking for a place to go. How do you go from that to killing a child?"

"I guess we don't know for sure," King said. "But we saw them a couple of times after that first visit. It's like, they're stalking us. They somehow got JZ to come out and..."

"It's them, all right," Misty said. "It's the only thing that makes sense."

"Then, what do they want?" Charlie asked.

"We have no idea," King said. "The only time we spoke to them was that day Wyatt had words with them, and they hardly said anything."

"This is unthinkable," Charlie said as he plopped down on his couch. Nervously, he started to put one ring on his finger at a time as he contemplated the situation. "Like Zagan all over again. I remember the last time Sim was here was to tell me Zagan killed Flip and that the fortress was under attack. But I thought those days were over."

"We all did," Misty said.

Charlie flexed his ring-studded hand. Then he sprang from the couch. "We're going to react appropriately this time. We're going to send men back to the fortress, and not sporadically like Sim had us do last time. A group of us, right now, and they will fill every square inch of that fortress if they have to, and they'll stay until we eliminate this threat, so we can make sure no more of us gets hurt. There is no reason anyone on our side should be dying, at this point. We're too strong. This is what I always feared, and it's why I told you all that perhaps coming to the heights—"

"No, Charlie," King said.

"The last thing we need right now are 'I told you so's," Misty added.

"Right," Charlie said. "I just can't believe JZ..." He sat back down in a shaken state.

"I'm going to bring Teddy to Mrs. Chandler, and maybe you and Misty can gather some people so she can get out of here with them. I'm sure Frankie and Malayah would go. They're dying to be in charge of your community militia, from what we were told."

"Yes," Charlie said. "They are. I just have a hard time seeing it. They grow marijuana for trade, but still, I don't how comfortable people will be to have marijuana harvesters in that role. But I'm starting to worry they may be right about our current community defense leader. It's too much to think about now. My problems. Your problems."

"It's all the same," Misty reminded.

"Right, well, first things first," Charlie said. "Misty, you come with me. King, we will catch up with you and Teddy after we get Misty on the road again with some people."

"See you soon," King said to Misty.

Misty rubbed Teddy's head. "Good luck, buddy."

"Eh, it's nothing," Teddy said. "I've been shot before."

King and Teddy proceeded to Mrs. Chandler's apartment, who in turn led them one building over to another apartment that she had outfitted with the tools needed to tend to the dental needs of the community. They had raided a nearby dentistry office to get some of the things they needed, but the practice was still a bit archaic. Mrs. Chandler was the nervous type, ill-confident in doing anything outside a cleaning, which, without electricity, basically involved her brushing and flossing the patient's teeth. She also had antibiotics with questionable effectiveness, and some tools used for extractions, but she warned patients that removing a tooth was not the simple procedure it was back in the day. Novocain had no long-term shelf life, and as such, the tooth simply had to be worked out slowly over the course of a however long it took with tools and no anesthesia.

King held Teddy's small hand in his own as he sat in the recliner, his body as rigid as a board. His eyes were full of water and his upper lip swelled from the infected tooth. He was at his most vulnerable and did not want to let go of King's hand.

King knew what he was to the younger ones with Sim gone. Maybe not even a shadow of the man in knowledge of problem-solving and tactics, but his body was large and assuming, so his physical presence dominated any room he was in, and his eyes never wavered from seriousness or conviction. King did not scare easily, and he was highly courageous. He was a formidable opponent to anyone who would mess with his family.

"No worse than being shot," Teddy said, remembering what King had told him.

"That's right," King said. "I promise you Teddy, you'll be okay. It may hurt like a bitch, but I'm not going to let anything happen to you. Never."

"Did you tell JZ that?" Teddy asked.

It was a low blow, but Teddy didn't mean it that way. King knew this, but he contemplated its impact. He had never pledged to any of the orphans that he would eternally protect them from harm or death. Maybe if he had, he would have done a better job at protecting the others that had died. He thought of Big Will, in particular, whose face he couldn't stop seeing in his nightmares, which he felt badly about, because his memories of Big Will should be nothing less than nice dreams.

He felt he could have done better. Could have done more for him, Sim, and JZ. He lived with their blood on his hands, and it was a scary thing to think about, not being able to protect the ones he loved.

"I never did," King said, water in his eyes. "I wish I had."

"Why?" Teddy asked, staring at him with uncertain eyes.

"Because if I had, I would have made some different choices. But we can't live in the past, Teddy. We can only learn from it. So, if I tell *you* that you will be okay, you will be, because I will do everything possible to keep you safe. Because you're my brother, and I love you."

"I love you too," Teddy said, squeezing King's hand.

"Love's a great thing in times like these," King said.

"In any times," Teddy responded. "My mom loved me."

King smiled and released Teddy's hand. He pulled up a chair close by and sat back with his hands behind his head. Until Teddy started squirming and howling. This wasn't like extractions in the old days. King grabbed his hands again, working around Mrs. Chandler while she went about joggling Teddy's tooth loose.

King soothed Teddy's pain with soft shushes, reminding him of all their wonderful memories and the plans for many more. Teddy's long hair was matted in sweat, and his body twitched while Mrs. Chandler worked.

"It's okay Teddy," King said. "Just think of women. They have to give birth, and from what I hear, it's the worst pain imaginable. Matter of fact, I hear there is a chemical in the brain that makes them forget how painful it is, so that they'll not be discouraged from having more children."

"Don't believe everything you read," Mrs. Chandler said out of the corner of her mouth. "Anyway, you want to know what the worst pain is?"

King waited for her to continue without invitation.

"It's not physical pain at all," she said. "It's emotional pain. The pain of losing someone you love so much that it's worse than being shot, stabbed, or having a tooth removed without anesthesia."

"It'll still always be worth the pain," King said, thinking most recently of JZ.

"I can't disagree," Mrs. Chandler said. "It's always been the same, just more of a luxury now. This new world has taught us the fragility of our relationships with others. I don't think that makes us love people less. It just makes us more appreciative of them while they are here."

As Teddy squirmed, Mrs. Chandler freed his tooth. King smiled when he saw her holding the blackened hunk of enamel and dentin, but when he looked back at Teddy, he was unconscious, slicked in a layer of sweat.

Mrs. Chandler smiled. "He'll be fine. He's just exhausted himself. Let him rest, and when he wakes up, we'll give him some antibiotics. To kill that infection."

"Can I have it?" King asked. "The tooth?"

"Sure," Mrs. Chandler said, handing him the tooth.

King took it and eyed it as if it were a precious jewel.

When Teddy woke up a few hours later, King told him how they would bring the tooth back to the fortress, where he could put it under his pillow and await the Tooth Fairy, who would bring him something in exchange for the tooth. It would be magical.

Over time, many teeth had been lost by the orphans, but Sim never involved the Tooth Fairy in the matter, no more than he entertained talk of Santa Claus or the Easter Bunny. Sim thought believing in such things would weaken them. He once told King that, based on their protocol, if Santa were to ever enter their house, they would have to kill him. If was a funny thought at the time, but King figured if they could believe and have faith in God, then they could also have fun with the Tooth Fairy.

When King told him his idea, Teddy smiled, and said he remembered those days of receiving money for his lost teeth, but he had forgotten all about them until King reminded him. He wondered what the Tooth Fairy would bring him since there was no more money.

You'll have to wait and see, my buddy. But it will be something grand.

Twelve

While Teddy's extraction was taking place at the heights, Baby lay on her stomach atop her bed back at the fortress, reading through one of Sim's journals. There was not one that could be considered mundane, because each entry was an outpouring of emotion. It was hard to tell, though, whether he wrote the journals to heal, cope, understand himself better, ask for forgiveness, or to record history so that others could learn from it. Perhaps he had written the journals for all those reasons.

The earliest entry she could find dated back to when he purchased the fortress. To read it was to meet a man she had never known—a shadow of the man she had come to love.

March 8

I did it! I can't believe it! Today, I stood outside my new house, which was once home to Father Howard and was built in 1850. It's like a fortress. Ironically, my new yard is where the former church was, and I have such fond memories of the old church and this place where I attended Sunday school as a kid. I was only seven at the time it burned down, but I remember that sad day and the excitement when the church was moved to a new location. The rectory building was sold off, and all these years later, it is now mine. The history is alive here. The inside is newly renovated. I never thought I would be approved for the mortgage, but I was wrong, and it is surreal owning such a place. Wait until Amanda and Sara see this. Amanda will have no doubts how serious I am about making this work. It's so big. Sara could get lost in it. We can have more kids and put in a pool. The sky is the limit. I'm going to surprise her next week and have them out to see "a friend's" beautiful new house, and then I'll tell her it's all ours.

I'm so excited. It's a new beginning. It has to be, because I don't want to lose them. I can't. Maybe I'll even throw in a dog.

The fortress.

He had called it such since the beginning. And from this one entry alone, you could see why he would never abandon it, despite all the schools, churches, hotels, malls, prisons, and office buildings that populated the area and offered far more space after the fall. It made their after-story that much more precious. Sim had history with this place that went well beyond his purchase of the rectory. Who knew? He never talked about it.

She continued to flip pages. He didn't write every day, but several times a week. She flipped ahead to try to find the entry about showing Amanda the house. She knew it had to be there, and she wanted to know how it went over with her.

March 10

I spent the last two days cleaning the house from top to bottom. It was a good workout going up and down the stairs from the basement all the way to the third floor. I put down some area rugs and put up a bunch of pictures that even complemented the color of the paint on the walls. I think Amanda will be pleased that it doesn't look like some bachelor pad. She probably won't even believe it was me who picked out the stuff. There is so much more wall to cover, though, which is fine because I'm sure she'll want to put her own touch on the place. I had hoped to furnish Sara's room before Saturday when they see it for the first time, but I don't know if I'll have enough time. I ordered the mattress for her bed, and it won't even be here until next week. Oh well, they'll just have to use their imaginations.

I have to admit, though, I am nervous. Amanda left the apartment with Sara a month ago, and it seemed like the final straw. I hope it's not too late. I guess it was a long time coming. I could have done better. I love her and I think she still loves me. I just have to be more present and not so distracted by life that I forget what matters most. It was so stupid to think I could have my cake and eat it too. Late nights with my Army buddies, extra hours at school, bumming around on the weekend.

I forgot what mattered. Amanda leaving with Sara was a slap in the face, but maybe she won't believe my goal to change.

I'm hoping for the best. Who wouldn't give love at least a second chance?

When Baby finished reading the journal entry, she closed the book and sought out Sky. She wanted company when she read the entry of how Sim had won Amanda back. From what Sim had referenced in the past, Amanda took the bait, but nothing would compare to hearing about it in Sim's own words. He most certainly wouldn't have missed writing about it.

Baby, journal tucked under her arm, found Sky in the library, herself reading from one of Sim's journals. She glanced up when Baby entered and as she pulled out one of the chairs from the table and sat down.

"Where are the boys?" Sky asked.

"Miracle and Yamil are downstairs with Leo and Ms. Betty. I've been keeping my eye out the windows, but I decided to take a minute to myself to read one of Sim's journals. I have the oldest one in the bunch."

"I was just reading through one myself," Sky admitted. "All of the entries in this book seem to be of the fortress days. Many things I had forgotten and was reminded of. It was a good idea for him to write it all down. We can share them with everyone and enjoy a look back at the old days. There was one story about Big Will when he first came to the fortress, and he wouldn't leave Gigi's side. He would sleep on the floor with her, curled up in the corner of the room every night for weeks before Sim could get him to start using the bed. Apparently, that's how Big Will survived before Sim found him...sleeping on the floor of a veterinarian's office eating dog food. Sad."

"I read about the day he bought this place," Baby said, patting the book as she had it glued to her chest. "He bought it for his wife and daughter. They left him for a month, and he bought the house to get them back."

"We already knew that," Sky said.

"But what you didn't know is that he was going to show them the house and pretend it was his friend's, but then surprise them by telling them it was theirs."

"Shut up!" Sky said with a smile. "Did he write about that day?"

"I don't know," Baby said. "I was just about to find out."

Sky jumped out of her chair and ran over to Baby's side of the table. Baby laid the journal out flat and turned some of the pages. She read a little, then turned a page. Read another, then turned the page. Finally, she found the page she was looking for and shouted, "Here it is!"

"Well, read it," Sky insisted.

March 15

It was an amazing day. Me and my friend Ray convinced Amanda to come for a cookout at "Ray's" new house. Of course, Amanda and Sara fell in love with the place and talked about how jealous they were of him, especially since they were living with her mother while we figured things out. When the grand tour was over, though, I broke the news, and she thought I was joking. She put her hand over her heart and her jaw dropped when she realized I had actually bought the house for us. She started crying, and it erased all doubt in my mind that she would say yes to trying to reconcile. Which was good because my heart was pounding. I told her I was sorry and didn't want to lose her and Sara, and that this fortress of paradise was for our new life and that I promised I wouldn't mess up again. She hugged me and I held her tight. Then, Sara ran all through the house looking at which room she wanted for her own, even though I had earlier picked one out for her. That didn't seem to matter. She picked out a room all on her own. It was a smaller room with low ceilings all the way up on the third floor. Then I brought Amanda to another room on the third floor that overlooked the bridge, the river, and the entire city.

I never felt so proud. She wondered how I afforded it, and I told her I hadn't yet, but only had a mortgage that I would have to work hard to pay, but that it was a good deal because even though it was amazingly beautiful, it wasn't in an upscale neighborhood. It was only two miles from housing authority complexes. But, still, our house made the others on the street look like shanties.

I won her back. I won them both back. I have another chance and I'm not going to ruin it.

This is our new life.

Sky and Baby gushed; they didn't know too much about the man Sim had been. They only knew the man Sim had become. The girls were excited to read more for memories lost and other things unknown about the man they loved.

JZ would have loved this story, and it was a shame, they thought, that she wasn't here to listen to it.

While the girls were pouring through Sim's pre-apocalypse life, Yamil and Miracle were in the kitchen putting dishes away. Ms. Betty escaped from underneath Leo long enough to pop into the kitchen and whisper to them.

It's time, boys.

Leo was fast behind her, and when she turned around, she nearly ran into him.

"Woah," he said.

"I was looking for Sky," Ms. Betty said, redirecting Leo to the front. "I think I may have seen someone out in front a minute ago."

"What?" Leo said, confused. He reached for his radio as he headed for the front windows.

"All right, listen, guys," Leo said. "Ms. Betty told me she thinks she saw someone out front. Where is everyone?"

Leo heard the trampling of feet above him.

"Third floor," Wyatt said. "Checking it out."

"I'm at the top," Jim said. "Taking a peek as we speak."

"Baby and I got the second-floor windows," Sky said. "Remember, stay put. If we see something, maybe we can take some clever shots from the fortress but stay clear of the windows."

While everyone gathered on their respective floors to the front of the fortress, Yamil and Miracle remained in the kitchen. Nobody was paying attention to them. It was exactly what Ms. Betty had in mind.

"Are you sure we should go?" Yamil asked.

"But Ms. Betty says," Miracle said. "Someone will take us to Sim."

"I know, but Sky will be mad," Yamil said.

"But if we find Sim, she'll be happy," Miracle smiled.

Miracle climbed onto the counter next to the sink, peered out the window to the backyard, and pointed his small finger.

"There he is!" the boy said excitedly as he pressed his face to the glass. His breath fogged up the space around his mouth and nose. "I see him moving."

"Let's get Sky and tell her that Sim has come back," Yamil said, clasping his little hands together.

"No, no," Miracle said. "Ms. Betty said we can't tell, or it won't work. Just me and you. She said it was the only way it would work."

"I don't want to," Yamil said.

"We can hold hands," Miracle said. "I see him right out there. We can come right back in and show Sim to everyone, and Sky will be so happy again."

Yamil, thinking twice, grabbed a kitchen knife that was lying on the counter and tucked it into his sock. It made him feel safer to have a weapon.

"Okay," Yamil said. "We have to do it quick."

Miracle hopped off the kitchen counter and landed squarely on both feet. He grabbed Yamil's hand and, with a huge smile, unlatched the door leading outside from the kitchen. Though it was made of oak and very heavy, he managed to heave it open. It creaked on its hinges, but not loudly enough that others would hear. The two slipped out to the porch together. The sun was shining, and the sky was blue, though dark clouds were visible in the distance. The willows in the backyard swayed gracefully in a gentle breeze. The boys stood on the back porch for a few minutes, staring into the yard, doubting their choice to leave, but excited at the hope of seeing Sim again.

"Maybe we shouldn't," Yamil said. "Sky won't like us to be out."

There will be a friend of mine, waiting. He will bring you to where Sim is waiting. And won't that be amazing?

"We can be quick," Miracle said. "I miss Sim."

Yamil felt a surge of nervousness in his stomach, like what he felt when scary things happened. Sky said not to leave. Sky said to be careful. JZ left, and she got hurt. It was not the right thing to do, but he was curious about Sim coming back like Ms. Betty said. Why would Ms. Betty lie? She was nice. She was their friend. She was only trying to help.

The two squeezed each other's hands and proceeded down the steps into the yard, intent on finding Sim and bringing him back.

Wasn't a quick trip outside alone worth it?

They skipped together to the back of the lot, near Usland, and stopped short of the wall, just where its construction ended. Behind it, there was a man with a friendly face who was waving them over.

Yamil hesitated, and it was Miracle that pulled him along as they rounded the wall where they were then concealed from the fortress.

The man, Pan, gave one last look at the fortress, and noticed Skinny Jim's back to the rear as he conducted a futile search for perpetrators at the wrong side of the house.

Good job, Ms. Betty.

"Where's Sim?" Yamil asked, pointedly. "We have to go back."

"Oh, children," Pan said, leaning forward and placing his hands on his knees. "Didn't Ms. Betty tell you that I was here to lead you to your friend, Sim? He's at a special place called Valley Hall, but it's not too far from here. And guess what?"

"What?" Miracle said, delighted.

"I was just talking to him before I came here, and when I told him that I was coming to bring you to see him, he was so excited."

Yamil and Miracle took a breath at the same time.

"But we must go, quickly," Pan said. "Your friends will be looking for you soon, and if they find you now before we have had a chance to get Sim, it'll ruin everything."

Pan held out both hands. They were bony, dry, and cracked.

The boys each took a hand, and Pan escorted them away from the fortress compound and started them on their journey to Valley Hall.

Back inside, everyone still had their eyes on the front, talking back and forth on the walkie talkies until they resolved that there was nothing out there.

"I've checked with the binoculars ten times," Skinny Jim said. "I don't see a thing."

Sky rushed downstairs with Baby on her heels. She approached Ms. Betty who was standing idle at the front window.

"What did you see, exactly?" Sky asked.

"I can't be sure," Ms. Betty said. "But it looked like a person. My eyes aren't what they used to be, though."

"I didn't see nothing," Leo shrugged.

"False alarm, then," Sky said. "It's better to be safe than sorry, I guess."

Just then, Gigi barked from the kitchen, which was never a good sign. Gigi rarely made noise unless she sensed trouble. Sky looked at Leo and Baby, and then they moved swiftly to the kitchen. Gigi was barking at the back door, which was partially open.

Wyatt came down the stairs from the third floor. "What's up with Gigi?"

"Where are Yamil and Miracle?" Sky asked suddenly.

She ran to the door and opened it all the way. Gigi immediately dashed out and ran across the back field. Baby and Leo followed.

"Wait!" Wyatt called. "It could be a trap."

Ms. Betty entered the kitchen. "Is something wrong?"

Wyatt picked up his walkie. "Eyes on the back, Jim!" he yelled.

Gigi didn't stop running at the edge of the property. She kept going. The others made it to the perimeter wall and stopped, out of breath.

"Yamil!" Sky yelled. "Miracle!"

"Oh no," Baby said. "Maybe they didn't come out."

Sky radioed to Jim who was scanning the back. "What do you see?"

"Same as the front," he responded. "Nothing."

"Wyatt, check the playroom!" Sky yelled.

This can't be. It can't be.

Baby and Leo were peering anxiously into the fields as Gigi's bark grew more faint.

A minute later Wyatt radioed back. "They aren't here, Sky. I called to them in the house. There's nothing. They're gone."

Sky saw JZ's body in her mind and started to hyperventilate thinking about finding Yamil and Miracle in the same state. Losing JZ was difficult enough, but the little ones? It wasn't possible that someone would harm them. And for what? They still had no idea who they were dealing with or what their motive was. All they had to go by was five mysterious men, one calling himself Vash. Was their goal to simply kill them one by one?

"This is a nightmare," Baby said.

"We've got to find them," Sky said.

"We can't go out there," Leo said. "They could be waiting for us."

"We don't even know who *they* are," Sky said.

"Exactly my point," Leo said. "We don't know what we're up against."

"I can't hear Gigi anymore," Baby said. "If she is chasing after them, then they aren't close anyway."

"This can't be happening," Sky said. "Not the little ones. Why is everyone leaving when they know how dangerous it is? What is wrong with us? Am I going crazy?"

Baby had no words that would ease the pain of the moment.

Sky wondered how things had gotten to this point. With the defeat of Zagan, she thought the worst was over, but it was clear the worst could be yet to come. She didn't know how she could possibly handle the deaths of Yamil and Miracle, even knowing they were all at risk, every day, little ones and all.

You have to be strong. You have to be strong. Keep it together.

"What's our move?" Skinny Jim radioed from the roof.

Sky, shocked expression on her face, did not respond.

Leo pushed his blue glasses up on the bridge of his nose and returned a response. "We'll wait for the backup from the heights and then organize a search party. In the meantime, keep your eyes peeled up there as usual, and if you see anything suspicious, notify us right away."

"Roger that," Skinny Jim said.

Sky protested. "We can't leave them out there."

Her eyes were desperate as she grabbed on to Leo.

"I...can't leave them out there," she said. "They're helpless."

She remembered that it was only days before when Leo reminded her how dependent the younger boys were, and how they needed to be trained and helped to understand the reality of the world.

"I just thought…if they could be little for a bit longer, they might feel…normal. Oh, Leo."

She leaned into Leo, and he embraced her, though he was several inches shorter. "You didn't know, Sky. We're all doing the best we can here. But there is little we can do to protect anyone if they are going to ignore protocol."

She pulled away from him and shuddered. "It's not an excuse."

"Still, there is nothing we can do at the moment, Sky," Leo said. "They're gone, and maybe God will bring them back to us. But they're on their own for now, if they're even still alive."

It was a brave thing to say, but it would not be realistic for any of them to think finding their bodies was out of the realm of possibility.

Sky sunk, her face defeated. Then, suddenly, she remembered the note left with JZ by her killers when they discovered her.

You will all march obliviously to your destruction.

Was it true? Would they all march to their deaths like fools? If so, why? Why did JZ leave? Why did Yamil and Miracle leave? Would they all leave to be slaughtered unwittingly?

As she considered these things, she saw Ms. Betty standing at the top of the deck stairs, peering out at them.

Ms. Betty. Who is this stranger we have in our home? Why did she stay instead of going to the heights? Was it not her who stole their attention away from the back side of the house?

"Leo," Sky said as she stared back at Ms. Betty. "Did you have eyes on Ms. Betty at all times in there before the boys went missing?"

"Yes," Leo said. "I've been up her butt since the day she came. And it hasn't been fun."

"When was the last time you saw Yamil and Miracle?" Sky asked.

"Two minutes before we all ran to the front of the house. Just before Ms. Betty told us she saw something."

"Where were you when she told you that?" Sky asked.

"In the kitchen!" Leo yelled.

"Let's get back, then," Sky said flatly. "I need to have a conversation with Ms. Betty."

The three of them walked in long strides back to the fortress. Ms. Betty waited for them to close the gap and offered a sympathetic stare from the porch as they returned.

"Are those sweet boys gone?" she asked. "Where did they go? It's not smart wandering off in these times."

It isn't smart, and the boys know that. They were tricked into going out by someone. Just like JZ.

Sky bit her tongue and held her suspicions about Ms. Betty close to her vest as she passed by the older woman and led the way for them back into the house.

Pan was pleased with the results of Ms. Betty's diabolical plan. He hadn't been sure if it would work, as he knew the residents of the fortress would keep a close eye on her. He was anxious, after receiving her note, to see who she'd be sending out to him to be the next victims of their cunning and subtle assault on the fortress. When he saw children so young, he knew his task would be made easy.

Ms. Betty had convinced them to leave the safety net of the fortress with the promise of seeing Sim brought back to them.

Pan did not see this story as far-fetched, as they were planning Zagan's return and believed they could see it through. The fall of the world—Armageddon—only cemented their church's belief that higher powers were at work, and that they would prevail in the battle for all that remained between God and Satan, with Satan's help and wicked intervention on their behalf.

Zagan would return, and their powers would increase tenfold.

As soon as Pan led the boys far enough away from the fortress, he tied their hands and feet and blindfolded them to render them helpless. Though they were confused, they did not struggle, for they couldn't. They were too small. Powerless.

Pan thought of his own children when they were as young. He was never able to raise them the way he wanted. And in the end, it didn't matter, because they died. He might never see them again, except on the other side of the spiritual fence.

He placed the boys in a rugged plastic wagon, which he pulled along the road toward Valley Hall. He thought of Ms. Betty remaining at the fortress and all the havoc she might continue to wreak while the orphans wallowed in ignorance of her untrustworthiness.

As he walked along the broken highway and closed the distance to Valley Hall, he delighted in seeing his brethren from afar, heading his way, back from their ritual and forward to the fortress to await their next moves.

When their paths crossed, the parties stopped.

"The spoils of Ms. Betty's wit," Pan said, while the others relished the capture.

"I never would have dreamed these orphans would fall so easily," Vash said. "It's a testimony that Satan's power is rising."

"Three of the residents of the fortress left to the heights today," Pan issued more to Balaam, who had nurtured discussions with the heights on their first day.

"No worries," Vash said, still nursing his arm in a sling. "As I said last time we met, their militia should soon be working in our favor as they flip the script up there. They will have their hands full. Too full to be of any help to the fortress."

Amon escorted the others away from the wagon and out of earshot of the boys, who were sitting passively inside.

"These boys are a large prize," Amon said. "Before their ultimate sacrifice, we should use them to leverage our position with the other residents."

"I fully agree," said Vash. "I can't possibly imagine the lengths the others would go to protect them."

"Then I will proceed to Valley Hall and tuck them away for now," Pan said. "What will *you* do?"

Vash smiled. "Now that I know we have something to barter with, I shall present myself at the gate and give them our demands. If they don't leave the fortress, we will send them a message from our little friends here." He looked back at the boys sitting in the wagon. "If they remain, we will continue to send them messages written in blood, until they can't take it anymore."

Pan returned the smile. "It's all coming together."

"It was meant to," Vash said.

"Ave Satanas," Amon said.

Thirteen

Vash had visited the heights on the day of Baby's birthday celebration.

Their sister community. Their support network.

Vash knew that if he had any chances of securing the fortress as his own, he was going to have to take the heights out of the defense equation.

When he set off on this journey, he did not know what to expect or have any ideas about how he might disrupt the heights' involvement with the fortress long enough for them to solidify their takeover.

He arrived on the perimeter unarmed and was greeted by a jittery guard, and immediately his wheels started turning.

"Hello, friend," Vash said. "I would like to speak to the person in charge of your community defense. I want to have a word with him or her."

"You're not giving the orders around here, stranger," the young man said.

"Forgive me. I only want to alert him to a potential threat headed this way," Vash lied. "Bring him to me and I will wait. I am unarmed and wish no harm to anyone."

The man looked at him skeptically but retreated anyway. Ten minutes later, a stout man, clean cut, with greying hair arrived, PTR-91 rifle in hand. His stare was icy.

"What's this about trouble headed our way?" the man said as he closed the gap between himself and Vash.

"Sorry for the false alarm," Vash smiled. "I only wanted to get your attention. The name is Vash. And you are?"

"Tony," the man said gruffly. "What do you want, mister? I'm in no mood for games."

"I can see that," Vash said. "I have a proposition for you. And assuming you are not in charge of this community, but in charge of the defense and offensive team, that makes you more in charge than anyone else. That, my friend, is why I want to talk to you, specifically."

"Why am I more in charge than Charlie?"

Charlie. Yes, we've heard this name before.

"Because you and your men, I'm assuming, are controlling more of the guns," Vash said. "And in this world, he who controls the guns, controls everything."

"Yet here you are, unarmed, trying to control this conversation," Tony said. Then he turned to his sidekick, the jittery young man. "Go take a walk."

The other guard left, and Tony remained.

"Now tell me," Tony said. "What is this *really* about?"

"Forgive me," Vash said. "I must be transparent, because I fear that if this conversation goes sideways my life could be in danger, so I had to park a sniper behind me about 100 yards in that nest of homes over there, just to ensure I could walk away if my pitch was found to be less than acceptable."

"You have a sniper aimed at me?" Tony asked, looking over Vash's shoulder.

Of course this was not the truth, but Vash had no idea what to expect from the conversation.

"Yes, but it is nothing personal, I assure you," he said. "And no harm shall come to you unless you make a move to strike me down. So, let's be calm, and just listen. If what I am about to say interests you, wonderful.

But if not, I shall simply walk away. No harm done, and we both live to see another day."

"Keep talking," Tony said.

"Tell me," Vash said. "Are you happy with your current leadership in Charlie and this network you have going here with the heights?"

"That's a loaded question," Tony said.

"Of course, it is," Vash smiled, displaying his set of pearly white teeth. "Okay, then, let me describe things differently, since it sounds like you could have an open mind," Vash continued. "You see, me and my friends are very interested in securing the fortress for ourselves. We have particular interests in the site which transcend the luxuries afforded by the home, but I don't want to burden you with those boring details. We thought that if you and your army of men, assuming that's what you have at your disposal, might consider a coup on your lovely community, perhaps it would be a win-win for both of us. You in charge of the heights, us in charge of the fortress. No network, just two factions working in the same area with their own interests at heart."

Tony's eyes turned upward. "Me, in charge of the heights?"

"Oh, yes," Vash said. "Do consider."

Vash watched, and he could see Tony processing a thousand thoughts through his mind at record speed.

"Well," Tony said. "We do complain a lot about Charlie and some of the others. I have strong connections with most of the men I oversee, and I think I could be a strong leader for the people. I have lots of ideas. They may not work for everyone, but maybe Charlie's time has passed."

"It happens, you know," Vash said. "Everyone sees his time come to an end if he waits around long enough."

"And I don't care much about that fortress, and those sanctimonious kids," Tony said. "They brought us hell last year, and we ended up in a huge firefight. One of our own was murdered. Charlie puts them before us all the time."

"Exactly," Vash said. "Imagine not having to worry about them anymore."

Tony locked eyes with Vash, and Vash could see in his eyes he had been sold. "So, you just want me and my men to yank Charlie out of bed and anyone else that would support him and exile them, or kill them?"

"Well, my friend," Vash said. "I have an uncanny feeling that members of the fortress could be visiting you soon. Perhaps a good time to reveal your intentions is after they arrive looking for help. Maybe some of your men could indeed come to their aid, if you know what I'm saying. Get your men into the fortress and keep Charlie here until our own coup is complete and we will send your men back to you, and you can continue your work here while we continue our work there."

"I'll take care of things on my end," Tony said. "But once your men are in the fortress, we don't want you creeping around here or changing the deal. And I'm not killing Charlie or any of those brats...if you want them dead, you can kill them yourself. I don't mind kicking Charlie's ass out, and if you have the fortress under control, it should be smooth sailing for us to do the same up here. I just want to make sure we're going to be separate, but equal."

"I wouldn't dream of spoiling such blissful estrangement from one another," Vash said. "All we want is the fortress so we can welcome an old friend back home."

Vash departed that day, hopeful that his plans would unfold in predictable fashion.

⸻◈⸻

When Charlie approached Tony with Misty at his side, there was urgency in his voice.

Tony had seen the orphans arrive and remembered what he had discussed with Vash. He had a couple of days to prepare his men and to choose his team. He had consulted with fourteen of the eighteen men from the defense committee who he felt comfortable would join his efforts to steal control of the heights from Charlie. These were men who often complained about Charlie's proclivities, perceived weakness, and his alignment with the fortress, which was believed by some in the heights to be an albatross holding them back.

"Tony," Charlie said. "We need you to spare five men to go to the fortress with Misty right away. They are under attack, and we need extra people there on defense. We'll need five others to go with King, as well, when he's ready, and that'll give them just under a dozen extras at the fortress until this threat abates."

"That'll leave the heights with less than fifty percent of our normal defenses," Tony rebutted.

"I'm aware of the statistics, Tony," Charlie said. "But the heights is not currently the target of an enemy force, and we have plenty of other people here who can step up if needed. So please prepare these men now, and Misty will lead them back."

Tony selected five of his fourteen men to follow Misty back to the fortress, and the six of them left soon after. Little did she know, they were all plants, thanks to the work Vash had done to thwart the fortress's efforts at finding support in the heights.

After Misty's departure, Charlie headed to Mrs. Chandler's dental unit to see how Teddy was mending from the extraction.

King provided Teddy antibiotics from Mrs. Chandler's stockpile once he woke following the extraction. King put the tooth on a piece of dental floss for Teddy, so he could wear it around his neck.

Teddy soon fell back to sleep but then woke up with a fever. Mrs. Chandler put a wet washcloth on his head and gave him some crackers to nibble on, since he was not in the mood for a substantial dinner.

When she left his bedside, she approached King, who was at the kitchen table in the apartment-turned-dental-office. He made eye contact with her, and her expression only added to his anxiety about Teddy not being out of the danger zone.

King remembered his promise to Teddy and pounded the table, angry that the procedure couldn't have just gone smoothly. He didn't want to leave Teddy's side, but he was also worried knowing they were needed back at the fortress.

Charlie entered the apartment as King pondered the situation.

"How's everything going here?" Charlie asked. "I sent Misty off with five of our defense team. We'll send five more with you when you're ready."

"Teddy has a fever," King said worriedly from the kitchen. "I can't leave him. What more can we do?"

Charlie walked over to Teddy where he lay on the couch. "He does look quite peaked."

"I doubled his dose of antibiotics," Mrs. Chandler said. "It's a waiting game."

"No," King said. "No. We are not going to just sit here and wait. If he doesn't improve, we need to have a backup plan in place. It's best we start thinking ahead."

Mrs. Chandler pulled out a chair from the table and sat across from him. "Charlie, don't you have other stuff back at your apartment that is more potent, with a longer shelf life? The ones we've been giving him are some all-natural type, made by a vitamin company. They must not be doing the trick."

"We've been giving him vitamins to fight infection?" King asked.

"I'm sorry, honey," Mrs. Chandler said. "I should have known better with an extraction like this."

Charlie picked up the bottle from the table that was in front of the couch. He examined it after putting on his reading spectacles. "Oh, hell no. I'll go back and get what we need. You may want to keep him lucid so he can actually take it once I get back."

Charlie was the resident pharmacist at the heights. He warehoused all the medications in his pantry, so it was rationed correctly and not abused.

As Charlie was about to leave, Malayah and Frankie came through the doors of the apartment.

"There you are," Malayah said. "We've been looking all over for you. Something is going down out there with Tony."

"We tried to warn you, Charlie," Frankie added. "I think the guy is going loco."

"What are you talking about, ladies?" Charlie said. "I just saw him a few minutes ago. He sent some of his men back to the heights with Misty. He seemed fine."

"Then why is he assembling out front with all his men as if there's a party going on in here?"

"What?" Charlie said.

Charlie went to the window and glanced out. Sure enough, Tony and a handful of other men had assembled outside.

"What are they doing?" Charlie said.

"Beats me," Frankie said. "We saw some of the others when we were coming in the front way. He split his team up. I'm telling you these *putas* are boxing you in."

"Won't that mean we'll be boxed in too?" Malayah said.

"Boxed in?" Charlie held up his arms to Tony outside as if to ask what was going on. Tony didn't respond, he only stared at Charlie through the glass.

"We have to get that antibiotic," King said. "Now. There is no later on with this, so find out what the hell they're doing."

"You're damn right I'm going to find out," Charlie said. "Follow me, ladies."

Malayah and Frankie followed, armed of course, and ready for action. Charlie led them out the side exit and around to the back where he approached Tony.

"What the hell are you doing, Tony?" Charlie asked. "We're all good here. Get your men to their regular posts."

"Sorry, Charlie," Tony said. "But your ship has sailed. It's time for new leadership around here, so go back in there with your fortress friends and consider yourself under house arrest until these new people in town take the fortress. Then you, and anyone else who is still stuck up your ass, can find another place to go."

"I knew this guy was playing games!" Frankie said, raising her gun. Just then, the other men from the front rounded the corner of the apartment building.

"Are you serious right now?" Charlie said. "What about the men you just sent with Misty?"

"Don't worry about them," Tony said. "I'm sure they'll help things to transition smoothly."

"Are you crazy?" Charlie yelled. "They are all children there. These men already killed one of them, and they'll kill the rest without batting an eyelash, Tony. And you think they're your friends? We've been together for over three years, and you would end it like this?"

Charlie felt helpless.

"It's nothing personal, Charlie," Tony said. "We don't want to hurt anyone, but if we have to, we will. We are at the point of no return now."

"It's never too late, Tony. We can leave now and catch up with them. This doesn't have to be how it goes."

"Go back inside," Tony insisted. "And when it's over, we'll see you out of this place."

Charlie looked to the other men in Tony's group for rescue, but none of them flinched.

Oh, my God. The fortress. The kids.

"Let's get back inside and think this over, ladies," Charlie said.

He then feigned leaving while he grabbed a pistol from his waistband and pivoted back toward Tony and opened fire with his weapon. Though he did not hit Tony, he hit the man standing closest to him, who fell down dead. Malayah and Frankie opened fire too as everyone ran for cover.

Charlie, Malayah, and Frankie ran back into the apartment through the emergency exit door.

"Why did you bring us back in here?" Frankie asked. "We're trapped in here."

"I'm not leaving King or Teddy," Charlie said. "We need to get them and get out of here so we can reach the fortress and warn them."

"You go," Malayah said to Charlie. "Me and Frankie will stay with King. You get to the others before they get to the fortress."

Charlie nodded. "Tell King I'll handle this."

Malayah nodded. She and Frankie laid down cover fire as Charlie took off running from the apartment. When he had gotten far enough away, they closed the door and ran back to the apartment.

When they got there, King was gone.

"Where did he go?" Frankie asked Mrs. Chandler.

"He went to get the medicine," Mrs. Chandler responded. "What happened out there?"

"Tony mutinied," Malayah said.

"Mutiny happens on a ship, babe," Frankie said. "This is a coup. This fool is trying to take over the heights."

"They better let King back here safe," Malayah said. "They've gone crazy out there."

"Why would they want to do something like this to Charlie?" Mrs. Chandler asked.

"Age-old tale, Mrs. Chandler," Frankie said. "Power and control."

"I don't think for one second they are planning to let us out of here once this fortress takeover is done."

"Hopefully, we won't have to worry about that," Malayah said. "Charlie will get to them first."

While Malayah and Frankie hunkered down with Teddy and Mrs. Chandler, King left the building and proceeded to building eight. He didn't know what was going on with Tony, but as he got closer to Charlie's apartment building, he heard gun fire from behind him.

Shit. What is happening?

He thought of Teddy and kicked into a sprint. He ran into Scooter along the way.

"Hey," Scooter said. "What the hell is going on? I heard gunfire."

"I need to get into Charlie's apartment for antibiotics for Teddy," King said. "I think Tony might be going rogue. I left before the gunfire, but I don't know what's going on for sure yet."

Story of the last few days.

"Maybe go check it out and see if you can help. I'll be right behind you."

"Sure thing, man. I got you," Scooter said, and he rushed off in the opposite direction.

King tried to open Charlie's door when he arrived, not expecting it would open, but hoping it would. He remembered what Sim had taught them about how to kick a door open.

Raise your toes and use the flat of your foot like an anvil in that sweet spot right next to the knob. One or two good kicks will separate it from the molding.

King raised his booted foot and followed Sim's direction. He threw a swift kick at the door's sweet spot, and it swung open with an explosion of splinters. King smiled, despite the situation.

He ran into the apartment and headed for Charlie's pantry. Teddy needed him. By now, they all might need him.

Fourteen

MR. FORD ENTERED THE in-school suspension room, where Charlie was sulking. Charlie, then twelve, couldn't look him in the eyes. He hung his head low as Mr. Ford took a seat across the table from him. "You smacked a kid upside the head with a piece of pizza?" Mr. Ford said. "Are you serious, Charlie?"

"I already heard this lecture before," Charlie said.

"It wasn't a lecture, Charlie," Mr. Ford said. "It was a rhetorical question. I already know what happened. But if I walked in here and pulled out a deck of cards and played war with you, it would make it seem as if I was okay with what you did."

"He called my mother a crackhead," Charlie said. "What was I supposed to do?"

"What I do when my Army buddies call me a coward and a bougie a-hole," Mr. Ford said.

Charlie then looked up. "Damn, even as an adult you get called names?"

"Oh, so you think people are jerks only when they're kids?" Mr. Ford laughed. "It *starts* when they're kids. Adults are worse because we expect them to be better than kids. But guess what? Doesn't happen. Better get used to it now, because ISS becomes jail, one day otherwise."

"Okay, what do you do, then?" Charlie asked.

"There is an expression, Charlie boy," Mr. Ford said. "Silence is golden. Sometimes, anyway. Pick your battles."

"You can't always just be quiet and not act," Charlie said. "Then people think you're a punk and that you'll let them get away with anything. It invites more aggression."

"Well, being a human nuclear reactor never solves anything either," Mr. Ford said. "You let people push those buttons on you like you are some sort of remote control...Then they will control you forever, because that's what you'll be."

"I'd rather be that than a standing target for bullies," Charlie said.

"Maybe, just maybe," Mr. Ford said, "you don't have to be either."

"And how do I do that, exactly?" Charlie asked.

Mr. Ford shrugged. "I don't know. But I'm sure we can figure it out." Charlie shook his head.

"Now, I said I couldn't just come in here and play cards without expressing my disappointment in your reactive nature, but now that I have expressed myself, what do you say we play some war?" Mr. Ford removed a pack of cards from his pants pocket. Charlie smiled, and the two played cards through Mr. Ford's lunch break.

Charlie thought of Sim, back when he was still Mr. Ford, his teacher, as he ran to catch up to Misty and Tony's treacherous friends.

He wasn't used to running and wasn't in the best shape, yet he knew the significance of trying to catch them. They had gotten a good head start, though.

How he could have put so much trust and faith in these people to have it end like this?

Truth is, he didn't care. He loved the heights, but his obligation to the orphans always came first. Sim had protected and guided him so much as a student. He was only their age when Sim showed *him* the way. He saved his life, in fact. Maybe not physically, but mentally. He couldn't repay Sim by failing him now.

He reflected upon the last seven months since Sim's death and felt pride. They had done well. This was only another challenge, like the one they had faced with Zagan. They would persevere. They would win. They were meant to win.

He ran the entire way to the fortress, except for when he needed to stop for breaths. He had hoped he would catch them on the road but realized when he reached the top of the hill that led down to the fortress that Misty and his men had gotten there first. He saw people out front whom he couldn't place, so he pulled offroad so they wouldn't see him. They were too far off for him to determine the situation, and it also looked like there were bodies in the road.

I'm too late.

Now what?

Something. Anything. Like when he, King, Willow, and Wyatt flanked Zagan's men from the hill during that battle, he might well be their saving grace this time as well.

He kicked into the woods and worked his way down the hill to the fortress after readying his handgun.

One way or the other, he was going to find out what was going on.

"You wanted me in the library?" Ms. Betty asked, her cheeks rosy red as she smiled ear to ear.

"Yes, I did," Sky said. "I wanted to ask you what exactly you saw in the front of the house when you directed our attention that way, when in reality, there was something going on in the *back* of the house?"

"Oh, dear, well," she began, folding her hands. "As I said downstairs, my eyes aren't what they used to be. Perhaps what I saw was someone passing from the front of the house to the back."

Sky regarded her with silence and a piercing stare.

"I understand how upset you must be losing your little friends—"

"They aren't my friends," Sky seethed. "They are my family, whom I deeply love. I'm going to find them and bring them back here, and if someone harmed them, so help me God, I will spend the rest of my days hunting them down and killing them slow."

"I'm sorry, Sky," Ms. Betty said. "I can see you're anguished."

"Tell me, what...you...saw...out front," Sky demanded.

Ms. Betty stared at Sky for several seconds, then grabbed a book that was sitting on the library table and threw it at her. It caught Sky in the face, and her head snapped backward as the book made contact.

Ms. Betty turned to run, but Sky recovered quickly and rounded the table. She tackled the old woman and they fell to the ground. Ms. Betty, more physically agile than she let on, elbowed Sky in the face and slid out from under her. She picked herself up just as Sky, too, got to her feet and once again forward tackled the woman into the second-floor stairwell banister.

Sky punched the woman in the face and kneed her in the groin. Ms. Betty wound up and punched Sky in the face, sending her backward into the library.

Sky bellowed, and Leo, Wyatt, and Baby came running. Wyatt came down from the third floor, and Baby and Leo came tearing up the main stairwell from the first floor. Ms. Betty ran for the back stairwell to the kitchen, but Sky once again jumped on her back, and the two tumbled down the winding stairwell and crash landed on the kitchen floor.

Baby and Leo went back down the main stairwell and ran around to the kitchen. Ms. Betty was struggling to get to her feet as Wyatt came down the back stairwell, which was blocked by Ms. Betty and Sky's bodies.

Sky recovered quickly and drove several kicks into Ms. Betty's side. She moaned and turned herself onto her back. Sky straddled her.

"Tell me where they are!" she screamed.

She slapped the old woman across the face to the right, then to the left. Ms. Betty spit blood from her mouth and laughed. Sky slapped her twice again.

"Where are they?"

Wyatt pulled Sky from the top of Ms. Betty and the group surrounded her.

"No, Wyatt, no," Sky cried. "She did this. She knows where they are. She knows what happened. Tell us what happened!"

Wyatt held her until she calmed down, while Baby and Leo stood there in shock over Ms. Betty's bruised and bloodied body.

"Scream," Ms. Betty said. "All of you, scream. The last sounds you will hear in this world are each other begging for your lives and your friends' lives."

"Let me at her!" Sky said as she tried to pull away from Wyatt's grip.

"He's coming," Ms. Betty cackled. "He's coming, and there's nothing you can do about it. *Ave Satanas.*"

"Who?" Leo asked. "Who is coming? What is going on here?"

She smiled a bloody grin. "Zagan."

"It's impossible," Sky said. "I cut his disgusting head clean off!"

"The body is but a vessel, my child," Ms. Betty said. "Zagan is not his body no more than you are yours. He *will* come back, and this place will become a lake of fire upon his return." Ms. Betty laughed. "A lake of fire!"

A gunshot cut through the air, and Ms. Betty's head split in two. Baby lowered the weapon as blood pooled beneath Ms. Betty's head.

"Baby!" Sky screamed. "She might have told us where they were."

"She wasn't telling us anything that was helpful," Baby said. "Let's throw her into the street, so when the others return, they can see her corpse. Let *them* be afraid for a change."

Skinny Jim radioed down as the gun smoke dissipated. "What is going on down there? Should I come down?"

Leo grabbed the walkie that was clipped to his waistband. "No, Jim. We've killed Ms. Betty. She wasn't one of us."

"Holy smokes," he said. "She bamboozled us good."

"She did," Leo said.

Just a little old harmless lady, eh, Leo?

"I did watch her, you know," Leo said to Sky whose chest was heaving.

"I know," she said. "None of us saw that coming. She could have poisoned us or found a gun and killed us in our sleep. It's a cautionary tale about letting transients in here. Something Sim was worried about since the very beginning."

As Wyatt and Leo were dragging Ms. Betty's body out the front door, Baby was cleaning the blood trail left behind. Sky handed Leo a piece of paper and safety pin so he could secure a note, composed by Sky, on Ms. Betty's body.

Once they had her removed, they tossed her into the middle of the road, then looked up to the roof where Skinny Jim was peering down.

Leo radioed up to him. "Keep an eye out. If anyone shows up, radio us. Do not fire without word from us down here. They may still have Yamil and Miracle."

"Roger that," Skinny Jim said.

"I'll be up to take over at nightfall," Leo said.

"It looks like we have our hands full of Zagan trouble once again," Wyatt said.

"These people are delusional if they somehow think they can bring Zagan back," Leo said.

"At least it gives us a sense of where their heads are at," Wyatt said. "Remember that Achilles' heel talk?"

"What weakness can we assume from a group of people that think they can bring Zagan's spirt back to life?"

"Well, let's give that some thought back inside," Wyatt said.

As they were headed in, Misty came down the hill with five people from the heights. They were all heavily armed and ready for business.

Leo and Wyatt smiled.

"Now we're talking," Wyatt said.

"You know those people?" Leo asked.

"One of them," Wyatt said. "Todd's a good guy. Can't vouch for the others. But if Charlie sent them, they must be good people."

Misty approached the body of Ms. Betty with a shocked expression on her face.

"She was a plant," Leo said. "Yamil and Miracle are gone. We think she arranged it."

"Gone?" Misty said, horrified. "As in…dead?"

"We don't know," Leo said solemnly. "Gigi went after them, but we haven't seen them. It looks like Ms. Betty tricked them into leaving the house. Those guys either have them…or worse."

The crew went inside to collect themselves and wait for what was next.

Fifteen

WHEN PAN GOT THE children back to Valley Hall, he led them blindfolded into their rooms, which were dank, hollow spaces with peeling paint, set up with a couple of mattresses and blankets. He sat Yamil down on one and Miracle on the other, then left them alone. During his brief departure, Yamil reached out to Miracle. "Ms. Betty lied," he said. "She's mean."

He heard Miracle whine.

Pan returned and made them each drink a glass of something, which tasted somewhat like water, but was bitter. The drink made them sleep, and within minutes they had fallen into unconsciousness.

After dark, Yamil woke up. He was drowsy. His blindfold had slid up over his eyes, and he spotted a light in the corner of the room he was in, but it was blurry because his eyes were still adjusting. He wanted to rub them, but his hands were tied behind his back. His feet were also bound together. He could feel as much, but he couldn't see his legs. He was on the same mattress he remembered sitting on when he was first put in the room.

He shuffled, turned, tossed, pulled, and squirmed to no avail. So he stilled his body and calmed his breathing.

As he recovered from the effects of the drug, he could see more clearly that the light source was a lantern set on a table in one corner, but there seemed to be little else in the room. The room was barren, with paint peeling off all four walls. It smelled pungent, and the cold air in the room burned his nose. There were lots of shadows on the wall behind him. They loomed large like black ocean waves ready to break on top of him and drown him. He peered around the room, squinting through the dark. He noticed another mattress on the ground with a lumpy shape on top of it.

Miracle?

It had to be, as he remembered hearing Miracle whining before he fell asleep.

Two grungy mattresses and four walls certainly did not make a bedroom. He missed his own bedroom, cozy and warm, which made him sad. He wanted to be home. At the fortress. With Sky and Sim and all his brothers and sisters. He wanted to cry, but he also wanted to be brave.

He remembered that before he and Miracle left the fortress to stay at the heights, before Zagan's attack, he told Sim how scared he was to leave.

I'm scared.

I am too, but you must be brave, Yamil, like you were when you went with me and left your mommy.

I don't remember.

You cried, much of the way to the fortress. When you looked at me, I saw the fear in your eyes, because you didn't know me. But you went anyway, even when I put you down for a rest. You held onto my leg when you could have tried to run.

I was scared?

Yes, you were. But you were brave, because you came with me anyway. You see, Yamil, being brave does not mean you aren't afraid. Being brave means, you are afraid, but you do what you have to anyway. It's acting in the face of fear. In this world, we must know how to act, even when we are afraid. That is why you need to go now to the heights. And when it's over, you will come home.

Yamil never saw Sim again after he hugged him goodbye that day. But he did come home, and he still felt Sim's love around him, and hoped so badly that the man would bring them to him, even though he didn't believe they would as much as Miracle did. They were tricked. Sim would never trick them. Only bad people would do that. Bad people wanted to hurt them. He had to escape. He had to protect Miracle.

As he struggled with his bindings, the door to the room cracked open slowly, and a shadowy figure entered, holding a second lantern. Yamil froze, pretending to be asleep, and he thought it could be working because the bad man at the door did not say anything at first. He only stood there quietly, and Yamil wondered what he was doing.

"Do I hear the sounds of little mice playing in here?" said the voice from the door. "I think I do."

It was the voice of the man who had led them away, who sounded so nice at first. Yamil felt that fear and he tried to ignore it. He tried to remain still and prayed that the bad man would go away.

"You know what happens to little mice that go for the cheese in the trap?" he whispered. "You will find out soon, and all hope will be lost. Then you'll all die in despair...and Zagan's burial ground will be ours."

The man backed away and closed the door. Yamil heard it click and breathed a sigh of relief. He didn't understand everything the man said, but some of his words were scary, and he was sure that the man was going to hurt him and Miracle. He hadn't yet, though. There was time. He had to get free.

He continued to struggle with the bindings. The man had heard him earlier, and he wanted to be quiet, so he rested again to think. He thought about how he could keep trying to get the ropes off.

Yamil rolled himself off the mattress onto the ground. His body hitting the grimy floorboards made some noise, so he waited a minute before he continued to wriggle his hands from the ropes. They felt like they were getting looser. If his hands were only in front of him, he might be able to see if they checked his sock for the knife he had put there before he and Miracle left the fortress. It felt like it was still there but his legs were tied too tightly together to know for sure.

He started to remember more things Sim had taught them as he concentrated hard on his training instead of being afraid.

He remembered the day Sim had gathered the orphans outside in the backyard for a group training. It was a hot, sunny day. He remembered Sim was in shorts, and he thought that was silly because Sim didn't often wear shorts. Not even when he took them to the creek to swim. His legs were white, skinny, and hairy. Yamil giggled.

You think my beach look is funny, huh? Well, what I'm about to teach you guys is not funny at all. It could save your life, whether you are wearing shorts or pants. Whether you are a girl or a boy. Whether you are young or old. You do not have to be snared by the fowler if you only listen to me.

Sim had Ace bind his hands behind his back. The orphans laughed, and Big Will yelled "charge!" and tackled Sim to the ground. Sim laughed as he lay in the bright green grass, his hands behind him, with five orphans on top of him tickling him until submission. Ace called them off, and Sim eventually showed them his trick.

Remember, my children, there is only one thing you must do when confronted with any problem in the world, and you can solve it most of the time. You must stop and think.

Sim then raised his legs into the air, so they were nearly straight up. Then he lifted his butt off the ground and pulled each leg through his bound arms. And seconds later, his hands were in front of him. He jumped off the ground and said, "Now come try me!"

He, Miracle, Big Will, Baby, Teddy, and Leo rushed toward him. And one by one he tossed them aside to the ground like rag dolls. Everyone was laughing under the warm sun.

Yamil rocked back a little and lifted his legs up, but they fell back down. He did it a second time and the same thing happened. On his third try, he was able to get his legs to stay up straight in the air, and then he pushed his rear end slightly off the ground. He pulled his arms forward and wiggled them around his rear until they came free, and when he dropped his legs, his hands were in front of him, still bound, but it was easier to move them around. He ripped off his blindfold and felt...free.

In that moment of triumph, Yamil smiled because Sim *was* alive. His echo. His love. His teachings. Without even realizing it, the bad men might have been telling them the truth about Sim coming back, because Yamil hadn't thought of Sim as much in the past seven months as he had since waking in the dark bedroom.

With his hands now in front of him, he reached for the knife he sleekly tucked away in his sock. And as he lifted his pant leg, he was elated to see it still there. The man might have thought they were too little to be clever. Too little to be carrying weapons. But he was wrong.

He grabbed the serrated knife and easily cut through the thin ropes binding his legs. He tiptoed over to the other mattress with the lump and knelt beside it. He swallowed hard, hoping it was Miracle and not one of the bad men. Instead of risking it, he went over to the corner of the room and grabbed the lantern from the warped and wobbly nightstand and quietly walked to Miracle's bed. He could see with more light that it was a small shape under the blanket.

He placed the lantern beside the ratty mattress and pulled back the covers. He breathed out hard and then placed his hand on Miracle's shoulder. He pulled the blindfold off the boy's face and shook him until he stirred and turned to face him. When he did, he smiled a one-toothed grin. He lost his first front tooth weeks earlier, and he teased Yamil that he was still a baby because he still had all his baby teeth.

"Did Sim come back?" he quietly asked.

Yamil quickly put an index finger up to his lips to warn Miracle not to make a sound. But he shook his head in answer to Miracle's question.

Yamil moved the covers off Miracle's legs and sawed through the ropes binding his feet. Miracle then rolled over onto his stomach and waited for Yamil to cut his hand bindings. When he was free, he pulled himself up and sat on the edge of the bed. Yamil handed him the knife, and Miracle went to work cutting the final bindings loose on Yamil's hands.

When the boys were free, they hugged, then Yamil stashed the knife back into his sock while scanning the room for a way out. Though most of the windows in the room had boards over them, he saw one that was uncovered, so the pair quietly went to that window and peered outside through shards of broken glass. The moon and stars were covered with clouds, and it was dark and spooky outside. The two boys looked at each other. Miracle looked anxious, and Yamil wanted to tell him the secrets he remembered about being brave, but he didn't want to make noise. Instead, he put a hand on Miracle's shoulder to assure him that it was going to be all right. Going outside would be scary, but staying in a place where bad men were going to hurt them was even scarier.

Yamil pushed upward on the pane and the window slid open. Miracle pulled himself up onto the windowsill, then jumped through the open space. Yamil watched as the night swallowed him whole, like the whale that got Geppetto. He turned back to where the lantern sat on the floor near Miracle's mattress and considered bringing it, but he reconsidered, figuring it could lead the bad men to them.

He did have one last idea, though, and ran back into the heart of the room. He put the lantern back in the corner and bunched up their bedding and blankets to make it look like they were still there. When he was satisfied that his trick could work, he dashed to the window and popped himself through. He landed on his feet, and Miracle was waiting for him. Yamil grabbed his hand, and the two ran toward the back of the old rundown building.

They fled into the yard, past some picnic tables and an area where there were lots of sticks piled in a heap. It smelt smoky, like the fireplace at the fortress. It reminded Yamil of home and gave him courage.

They entered a wooded area behind the open spot and had to slow down to avoid colliding with bushes or tripping over fallen logs. It was hard to see, and Yamil wondered if leaving the lantern behind was the best idea. There seemed to be no clear path that would make passing through the area easy, so Yamil had to push branches and shrubbery out of the way so they could get further.

"What happened?" Miracle asked. "We had a wagon ride, then fell asleep?"

"We have to keep going," Yamil answered. "We can't talk about that now."

"I want to go home," Miracle said.

"We are going home," he said. "But we have to go fast so the bad men don't get us."

"Who are the bed men?" Miracle asked.

"Ms. Betty and the one who took us," Yamil said. "He brought us here and wants to hurt us."

"I just want Sim," Miracle said. "He was going to come back."

Yamil ignored him as he forged ahead, pulling Miracle along. Once they got deep enough, there was less to push through and more openness. He thought about the woods near the fortress. He had never been in them at night, but he remembered what they looked like in the daytime. He pretended they were going to the creek for a swim and that the fortress was nearby. This helped him get further. He tried to make sure he was taking them in a straight line, so they didn't end up back in the bad place.

Sim had taught them how to use a compass and to tell directions by the position of the sun, but the sun wasn't out, and he didn't have a compass, so all he could use was his own mind.

The woods were full of life, with the sounds of crickets, frogs, and other small creatures rifling through the debris on the ground. Sim would take them out at night in the yard to listen to the sounds so they could become familiar with the noises they might hear and not be afraid of them. He pointed out the sounds of the peeper frogs, owls, bats, squirrels, rabbits, deer, and raccoons. So many things that had lived while humans died. One time they even saw a skunk waddling along in the backyard; it was small and fluffy, and if not for the threat of being sprayed, Yamil would have pet it.

There's nothing out here that will hurt you more than other people. Remember that.

It made sense. Their home was the fortress, and the fields, woods, and forests were home to all the creatures that stirred in the night.

"I'm hungry," Miracle said as Yamil pulled him along.

"I don't have no food," Yamil said. "We can eat later."

Yamil kept his focus on the path ahead, which he was carving steadfastly through the wooded area. He had no idea where the path would lead, but if it took them in the opposite direction of the bad people, then it would be enough in daylight. Maybe then, they could find a house to go into and find some food or something else that might be helpful.

He had never gone on a mission with the older kids, and he always wanted to. He asked once, and King told him he was too little. Leo would have let him, because Leo thought he and Miracle were too babyish. Leo wanted them to grow up and use weapons and see the world with their own eyes. But everyone else just thought they were babies. Nobody thought that something like this could happen. Even though it happened to Flip and JZ. They still didn't believe it.

Sim always tried to tell them that danger was everywhere. That in a world without rules, lots of people would be their true selves. And that was bad, because whatever people hid about themselves in the old world because they were afraid of punishment, they could unleash in the new world, where there were no time-outs, no going to bed early, no having video games taken away for a week, and no getting in trouble with the principal.

Yamil got them out the other side of the wood and onto some sort of back road. The sky offered little light because of the cloud cover, but he could see the outline of trees on both sides of the road. It was a relief to be on a road and out of the woods, but Yamil was scared that being out in the open would mean they were easier to spot. Even though he had never gone out on a mission, he was always there for Sim's lessons.

Try to keep yourself hidden or out of the way as much as possible. Use cars, houses, mailboxes, backyards, and trees for cover, and be in the open as little as possible. Especially in daytime. Avoid open roads and being in places where there is only one way out. Have eyes in the back of your heads. Move like your life is on the line every time you set foot outside this compound. Because it is.

Yamil looked up and down the unpaved road as Miracle sat on the pebbly surface beside him, exhausted.

"I'm cold," Miracle said.

It wasn't all that cold, but it wasn't all that warm, either. It was only middle spring, so the hottest weather had not arrived and the nights were chilly. Though uncomfortable, the weather was not a threat to them. Yamil did feel a few drops of water dot his skin, and he hoped with all the clouds in the sky that they weren't about to get dumped on.

"Okay, we will walk down this road while it's dark, but if we see a light, or when the sun comes up, we have to go back to the woods."

Yamil helped Miracle to his feet and Miracle whined. That's when Yamil said, "Stop it!"

He had never spoken to Miracle in such a tone or asserted any authority over him. They played together, slept together, ate together, and did chores together, but they always functioned on an equal plane. They rarely fought or argued, but their life together was never complicated. Now it was, and Yamil realized that Miracle's attitude would only slow them down and make them an easier target.

"No crying!" he said, pointing a finger sternly at Miracle. "We have to walk if we are going home. We will find food when we can."

Miracle nodded, his large brown eyes conveying a sense of understanding and guilt. The two walked the road downhill, not because walking uphill would be harder, but Yamil figured the downhill path would lead them back to a larger road. He had no idea where he would go from there. As the two walked, Miracle two paces behind, Yamil wondered how he would ever get home because he did not even know where they were, and he had never been out in the city before to know where anything was. He knew the river and the bridge from seeing it from the windows and roof. So he was thinking they could find the river, and it would lead them to the bridge.

As they continued down the road, the rain started to pick up, but it mattered little, because there was nowhere to go except for back into the woods, where at least the trees would provide some shelter. Eventually, he hoped they could cross paths with a house where they could shelter while it rained.

When the rain was coming down thick and heavy, Yamil led them back into the woods, but they stayed close to the road as they continued forward. Miracle didn't complain, but Yamil knew he was unhappy and miserable. So was he, but he couldn't stop. He knew, even if Miracle didn't, that their lives were on the line.

With the rain teeming, the downward path came to an end, and Yamil arrived at a corner where the woods continued right alongside a broken paved road with a yellow line in the middle. Or he could cross the side road at the opposite end and continue left, as the woods bordered the paved road on that side as well. Since he had no idea which direction was best, he decided to take them right, to avoid crossing in the downpour.

He and Miracle were hugging themselves to keep warm. Their clothes were soaked, and their hair dripped with water. They were shivering, and with each step, the water squished around in their shoes.

They trudged on in the night, slowing down to a crawling speed because they were tired and cold. Yamil kept thinking that anything was better than being tied up and prepared for whatever unknown fate awaited them at that place. What would the bad man think when he saw that they were gone? He would come looking for them. If he found them, he would take them back. Yamil didn't even know what the man looked like. But he did remember the scary men that came to the fortress on Baby's birthday. It was probably them. Ever since they came that day, Sky was hearing things, and Teddy heard things too, just like they did.

Tricks and lies.

It must have been two hours into their journey when they finally came upon a wooden house with a fenced-in front yard. It wasn't a neighborhood. Just some random house on the side of the main road. There was no firelight inside, or any other kind of light like the ones they had at the fortress that worked with batteries. It was dark. That didn't mean nobody was in the house, but Yamil knew they would have to take a chance.

They walked around to the front, and Yamil turned the golden doorknob. At first, he didn't think the door was unlocked, but when he pushed it with his body, it moved inward. A musty smell escaped, and Miracle and Yamil plugged their noses. Yamil reached down and pulled the knife from his pant leg. If anyone was in there, he surely would use it if he had to, but this house seemed to be abandoned.

The pair entered, and it was dark as the night. Yamil could make out some shapes as his eyes adjusted, like furniture. Once they were fully inside, Miracle closed the door behind them. It was cold inside the house, but at least there was no rain. Yamil led them through what seemed like a living room, stepping carefully so as not to collide with anything. Walking through the house was as unpredictable as walking through the woods.

Yamil knew by touch they were alongside a couch. It felt like the couch at the fortress. He directed Miracle to sit down and wait for him, and Miracle shimmied over to the couch and sat while Yamil made his way deeper into the home.

Off to the right of the living room, in the back of the house, he discovered the kitchen. He went about opening the cabinets to find something to eat, but he was not sure what they might find that would be any good at a house that had been abandoned for so long. He wouldn't find fresh fruits or vegetables. But he remembered Sim telling them in his scavenger trainings to look for canned goods.

He felt around, and his fingertips discovered dishes, glasses, bags, boxes, and cans, but he had no idea what was in them. On one of the cans, he felt a pull tab on the top, so he took it down and popped the top. He smelled the open can but still couldn't tell, so he dipped a small finger into the can, and it sank in a cold, thick, syrup-like liquid. As he swished his finger around in the can, he felt beans. He made a hook with his finger and scooped some up and reluctantly put it into his mouth. Thankfully, it wasn't that bad. Baked beans. Cold baked beans.

Yamil walked to the refrigerator with the beans in one hand. He opened it up with his free hand but quickly closed it as a waft of rotten air reached him. He decided, for the moment, the beans would be enough. He felt his way back into the living room and the couch, where he noted Miracle had sprawled out and fallen asleep. He was shivering in his sleep, so Yamil slipped his friend's sneakers off, followed by his jeans, and then pulled his sleeping body up into a seated position and worked his shirt off as well. He found a blanket draped over the top of the couch and used it to cover Miracle's trembling body after lying him back down. He spread his clothes out on the floor so that they could dry.

He did the same for himself and then found another chair nearby and sat in it. He ate some of the beans while he listened to the sound of the rain pelting the roof of the house. He heard some of the water dripping in from the roof in some other area of the house, but the living room was dry, so he was content. But even at seven-years-old, he knew they were not completely safe. If there weren't many houses in the area, the bad men might assume they went to the first house they could find and come looking for them there. Yamil knew that as soon as the sun rose and they peeked around the house for more supplies, they had to leave.

He wasn't sure where they would go next, but he knew it was on him to figure it out.

You see, Yamil. Being brave does not mean you aren't afraid. Being brave means you are afraid, but you do what you must anyway.

Sixteen

King rushed into Charlie's kitchen and opened a pantry door. The shelves were lined with dozens of pill bottles of assorted colors, vitamins, protein powders, ointments, and many other staples one might find in the pharmaceutical section of any store back in the day.

King struggled to remember what Sim had given to Ace when he was injured by one of Zagan's marauders during the probing attack.

It's starts with D. Dox...something.

"What the hell does he need?" he asked himself.

He discarded pill bottle after pill bottle to the ground looking for a label that sounded like the correct name. He would know it if he saw it.

He remembered Sim mentioning Amoxicillin. But Sim said the other one was better. As he continued to discard boxes and bottles in a frenzy, he finally came across the one he was looking for. He read it back to himself.

"Doxycycline Hyclate."

He did an arm pump.

This is it! I found it.

He fled back through the broken-down door, through the hallway corridor, and out into the yard. He dashed across the green grass, and as he got nearer to Mrs. Chandler's apartment, he saw an unexpected scene. Scooter was lying on his back with bullet holes in his chest and head. His eyes were open, staring into the sky.

It's for real. Charlie's men are trying to kill us. Why? What is happening? Has everyone gone mad?

King wanted to stop, but he couldn't, even if it meant risking his own life. Teddy wasn't going to make it without the medicine.

He pressed ahead, and as he closed in on the apartment, there were two men pointing guns at him. King raised his arms.

"I'm not armed!" he yelled. "My brother is in there and needs medicine or he'll die." He shook the hand holding the pill bottle and it rattled. "Please. Just let me in."

One of the men radioed Tony. "We have one of the fortress people here looking to get back into the apartment. He's got medicine for the other one."

"Let him pass, but if anyone tries to leave, kill them," Tony said.

The man flagged King forward. "You heard him. You guys are to stay put until we say otherwise. And give us that gun."

The men stripped King of his weapon before permitting him to move forward.

King had no idea what was going on, but he figured he would find out once he got back inside. He had heard the gunfire and saw Scooter dead, and he hoped that Charlie was still alive.

When he returned to the apartment, Teddy was unconscious and Charlie nowhere to be found.

Mrs. Chandler was kneeling next to Teddy, holding a cold compress on his head. Teddy was squirming and moaning, and not at all lucid. His face was red and slick with sweat.

"His fever spiked while you were away," she said. She handed Malayah the washcloth that was on his head. "Can you go run this under cold water, please."

Malayah took the cloth and ran off to the sink. Frankie stayed at a distance, quietly observing.

"I got these," King said, thrusting the pill bottle in her face.

Mrs. Chandler grabbed the bottle and placed it on the end table. "He needs to have his wits about him before we can give him these."

Malaya returned with the cloth and Mrs. Chandler pressed it to his head.

"When is that going to be?" King asked.

"If—When his fever breaks," Mrs. Chandler said.

King caught her slip up and ran his hands through his hair as he spun around in circles feeling hopeless. "Where did Charlie go? What's going on around here? They killed Scooter. He's out there lying on the ground with a bunch of bullet holes."

"What?" Mrs. Chandler clutched her chest. "We heard the gunshots but...Scooter? Who would want to hurt Scooter?"

Mrs. Chandler was horrified.

"Charlie ran off after Misty and the group," Frankie said, without her usual flare. "Tony seized control with his men. The people he sent back with Misty were plants. They are working with some group that wants to supplant your people at the fortress."

"Oh, my God," King said. "They're all in danger, and here I am again at the heights, surrounded by gunmen, and Teddy..."

"Let's just hope Charlie catches up with them," Malayah said.

"I'll take over," King said as he relieved Mrs. Chandler at Teddy's bedside. She still seemed to be grappling with the fact that Tony and others killed Scooter.

He placed his hand on the cold cloth, and it had already gone warm. "Go get a bowl of cold water so we can keep this thing cold."

Mrs. Chandler moved toward the kitchen, but Malayah held up her hand. "It's fine, ma'am. You've done enough for now. Take a break. You don't look so good."

Malayah answered King's call as Frankie continued to watch, stone-faced.

King grabbed Teddy's limp hand and squeezed it as he kept pressure on the compress.

How did this happen? He was just fine earlier today.

"Hey, buddy," King said. "It's me…King. I'm here. Like I said. I wasn't going to leave you. And remember, I said everything was going to be okay. I meant it. It's just a nasty fever, but you're strong. Probably stronger than me. You stayed that day to fight, and I ran. You were shot, and our brothers and Sim died."

Frankie watched as Malayah placed the bowl beside the couch. King trembled. His hand shook nervously as he dampened the cloth in the cold water.

"Anyway, it should be me there," he said. "You did everything right. You're a hero. Please. Don't leave me."

Teddy stopped squirming, but his color was pale and his body burning. King could feel the heat rising from his skin.

King looked to the others, desperate. "Should we put him in a cold bath? What can we do? What more can we do?"

"I'll go get cold water for the tub," Malayah said.

As she stepped toward the door, Teddy seized. His body convulsed and his muscles tightened. He started to make weird sounds and drool came from each corner of his mouth. King moved to hold him down, but Mrs. Chandler shouted.

"Don't hold him!" she yelled. "Just make sure he doesn't fall off the couch."

King watched in horror as Teddy's body arched and recoiled several times and his eyes rolled to the back of his head. Everyone stood helpless as Teddy's small body lifted and fell several times before it finally came to rest. And as it did, Teddy let out a large breath of air, but King noticed he didn't breathe air back in.

"Teddy?" King said.

He shook Teddy's skinny arm, which fell limp over the side of the couch. King leaned over Teddy's mouth to listen for breathing, but he heard nothing. He then felt Teddy's neck for a pulse, like Sim had taught him, but he felt nothing.

"No, no, no," King said. "I have to get him off the couch."

"King," Malayah said.

"I have to move him!" King said.

You see these dolls, children? They aren't just here to be cuddled. They are here to be saved. You see, when you save someone by breathing life into their body, it's a miracle. Maybe one day, someone will save you, or you may save someone with the techniques I am about to show you.

King and the others watched as he positioned the doll's head back to open the airway. He then placed his mouth over the doll's mouth while pinching her nose. He breathed two breaths. Then, with taut arms, did thirty compressions. Then, two more compressions. He continued for several cycles before relaxing.

You see, children, she's alive now.

She still looks dead to me, Teddy had said.

No, Teddy. She is alive, because you kept at it until she breathed again. You see, when the heart stops, it may take your heart and soul to bring it back to life.

After his demonstration, he invited each orphan to try before showing them the Heimlich Maneuver.

It may be a lot to remember, but when the time comes, it'll all come back to you.

Frankie and Malayah rushed over and moved the coffee table out of the way. King scooped Teddy into his arms and rested him on the ground. He tore the blanket away from Teddy's body and positioned himself over Teddy's chest and began administering downward thrusts, silently counting under his breath. Intermittently, he stopped to administer rescue breaths. Teddy's chest rose and fell with each puff. King continued his efforts in cycles, periodically checking for a pulse with shaky hands.

"Wake up, Teddy!" he cried. "Wake up!"

Mrs. Chandler stood in the corner with her hand over her mouth while Malayah and Frankie hovered over his shoulder, a look in their eyes as if they had been defeated.

King grew exhausted but wouldn't stop. He kept going even as his muscles tightened and started to ache. As he slowed down, Malayah reached for his arm to tempt him to stop, but King pulled away.

"We're going to do this all night," he said. "We're going to do this. This will work. It's *supposed* to work."

He continued two more cycles before yelling, "Teddy!"

After two more rescue breaths, and amidst a sense in the room that King's efforts were futile, Teddy rose halfway off the floor and drew in a large breath. King reacted in disbelief, for even he didn't think Teddy would come to. He immediately started to cry as he hung his head over Teddy's chest while Frankie, Malayah, and Mrs. Chandler let go of their own breaths and shrieked in relief, which gave way to happy laughter.

King released his arms from the floor and gently let his body fall into Teddy's. As his head lay next to Teddy's, he heard the boy whisper. "Did the tooth fairy come yet?"

Everyone in the room burst out in laughter, and King released Teddy from his embrace and picked him up. He placed him gently back onto the couch, and had Mrs. Chandler fetched him some of the new medication. Malayah brought several bottles of water from the kitchen, and they treated Teddy with wet cloths and made him drink.

An hour later, Teddy's fever was under control, and the new medication was coursing through his body. As King watched him sleep peacefully, he battled with his other dilemmas.

Charlie was betrayed by his own people.

Misty was in the company of dangerous men who were on their way back to help the group who killed JZ take over the fortress.

He was trapped. But even if they weren't, Teddy was in no condition to go anywhere, and he certainly wasn't leaving him behind.

Malayah and Frankie sat with King after Mrs. Chandler departed peacefully through the gauntlet of armed men that were keeping them from leaving.

Where are you going?

I'll be back.

It's dangerous out there. You should probably stay.

This is my home. There is no way in hell Tony and his goons are going to keep me prisoner.

Be careful.

As I said, I'll be back.

With lanterns burning, Malayah and Frankie each took a chair in the room while King sat on the floor, his back against the couch on which Teddy slept. Every few minutes, King looked over at Teddy's chest to make sure he was breathing.

King noticed Frankie and Malayah's curious eyes on him as he monitored Teddy's condition.

"We've been through a lot together," King said.

"You don't have to explain anything to me," Malayah said. "I think it's sweet. It's hard to find, nowadays."

"What?" King asked.

"Love," Frankie said, eyeing Malayah with a smile. "It went out with the birds. Or the virus."

"But Sim always told us that's why we have to bring it back," King said.

"I wish I had met him," Frankie said. "I saw him a couple of times when he came here, but I never really knew him."

King leaned his head back and felt it come to rest on Teddy's thigh. He stared into the ceiling. "When he rescued me, I was in the back of a car, not knowing what the hell I was going to do." He snickered. "I thought he was some weirdo guy...like so many others I met when I ran away from home. Truth is...I never knew too many good people, even before. My Dad and Mom were good, but then Dad died, and Mom changed...Everything changed. Until Sim...I had given up, I suppose."

Malayah and Frankie reached for each other's hands.

"But when someone teaches you to love and care," King said. "You want that feeling to last forever. You want to *give* that feeling."

"Well, we are in quite the situation, now," Malayah whispered. "I never did like Tony, and he sure as hell never liked me or Frankie. But still, I never expected this."

"I can't believe they killed Scooter," King said.

"It shows you what cowards they are. Scooter was harmless," Malayah said. "But if they'll kill Scooter, they'll kill anyone."

"But they let *you* back in," Frankie noted.

"I think Scooter might have come in guns blazing," King said. "He was running toward the gunshots. He never had a chance."

"So we just sit here?" Frankie said. "Until what?"

"You heard them," Malayah said. "They're keeping us in here until the fortress is seized."

"That isn't going to happen," King said. Though he wasn't sure if he was in denial or if he really believed it. "My people aren't stupid. Sim trained us to be anything but. These guys think they're setting a trap, but they're going to be walking into one. Let me tell you that much."

"Plus, you got Charlie after them now," Frankie laughed. "Once you fire that crusty old bird up, there's no stopping him."

"Yeah, this mutiny gonna come back to haunt these guys," Malayah said.

"How many times do we have to tell you that a mutiny is what happens on a ship?" King said.

"Well, sue me," Malayah said, crossing her arms with a huff. "You know what I mean, anyway."

"So, that's it, then?" Frankie said. "We just sit here and let these guys keep us under house arrest?"

"I don't know," King said. "What do you want to do? If Teddy were well, we could blast our way out of here. But when he's like this, we can't do a thing. Christ, he just almost died. I can't move him until I know he's recovered enough, and if I let you blast your way out of here, I'll be stuck to try and get both of us out on my own."

"I just hope Charlie is able to catch up with those *cabrons*," Frankie said. "Maybe Teddy will be all right in a few hours. But it's been nice chatting with you, King. Even under the circumstances."

"You too," King smiled.

"Well, if you want to catch an afternoon nap, we'll watch your little Teddy-bear here while you doze," Frankie said. "He's a cutie all the way to the bank. You done good saving him. I was like...whoa. Someone needs to teach me them skills."

King smiled with pride. He saved Teddy. He breathed life into his body when there was none there. For all the guilt and pain he felt over Big Will and Sim's deaths, he felt relieved to have finally done something right.

But there was more to do.

Seventeen

Dear Diary,

We have seen better days. Yamil and Miracle have gone missing, and I pray they are still alive. I must find out where they have been taken and find them. I can't just sit here, especially now that we have reinforcements. But where should I look? It's in these dire times that family means everything.

I miss you, Mom. I miss you, Dad. Uncle Mike...I wonder if you are still out there. I remember when you left me. If you were still alive, wouldn't you have come looking for me? You knew where I was going. One day, I might need to try and find out what really happened that day. The mystery of it haunts me still.

Anyway, I can't write much now, as we must remain vigilant. These men that mean us harm will return. And now we have an idea of what they want. This place, of course. How selfish of anyone to want what we built. But they would discover that even with this place, they would not have captured what the fortress truly is. Others think it's a building, but they don't know the truth. They don't understand the fortress of the human spirit.

In the end, this is what will win the war, even amidst losing battles.

Stay strong, boys. We are coming for you.

Sky, sitting on the living room couch, put her notebook aside just as Skinny Jim radioed from the roof.

"We have incoming," he said. "Three people."

Everyone rallied to the front of the house. Wyatt fled to the second floor with one of the men he was acquainted with from the heights, named Todd.

Everyone else in the house hung tight while they watched three men approach and stop at Ms. Betty's body, which had been placed in the street. The three men stood over her, appearing solemn. The man named Vash, sword neatly sheathed at his side, pulled a note from her body. Only Sky knew what it said. And when Vash read it, she felt a guilty sense of satisfaction.

Ms. Betty marched obliviously to HER destruction.

Vash, unamused, looked at the fortress with a piercing stare.

"It looks like they want a conversation," Sky radioed to everyone.

"How'd they know we wouldn't shoot on sight?" Wyatt asked.

"Because they know we are aware of the bargaining chips they have," Sky said.

Yamil. Miracle. They are still alive.

"That's a good sign, I guess," Wyatt said.

"I'm going out," Sky said. "You went the last time. Now, it's my turn."

"Be careful," Wyatt said.

Sky went to the main doors, and Baby opened one of them for her. Baby took up position behind Sky, who had her rifle aimed at Vash. The other two, Amon and Balaam, remained still alongside Ms. Betty's fallen body.

"So, you're back," Sky said. "We thought you might want Ms. Betty's body, so we left her out here for you."

"We felt the same way about JZ," Vash asked. "Which is why we left her tied to a tree for *you*. She was a delightful girl. Quite a fighter, too. Impressive."

Vash put a hand over his bandaged ear while Balaam placed a hand over his injured arm.

"Wow," Sky said. "Good for her. You don't look in any condition to fight."

"But we don't wish to fight," Vash said. "This was never about fighting. No, this was strictly killing. At first." He held up a finger. "A tale of revenge as old as the stars—for killing one of our people, Zagan, as I'm sure you could appreciate. He left us behind at the temple in haste and got himself caught up here in quite a debacle. But I don't know that he could help himself. You see, he might not have realized it, but this place was calling to him all along. It calls to us. All we want is to have your blessings in allowing us to occupy it, and you can all walk free, and we will forget this silly quest for revenge. We will even tell you where to pick up your precious little ones, who are quite a joy, by the way. They are, in fact, not too far from here."

Sky considered the irony of the situation when Zagan had showed up with Flip at their doorstep, promising to leave if they delivered Kellogg to them.

Never make a deal with the devil.

"Ms. Betty already told us where they are, and we have a party on the way to retrieve them," Sky said.

"Ms. Betty," Vash said. "It does come as quite a surprise that she would, in her plight to save herself, squeal about Valley Hall, but I don't believe you have anyone going there, or you might have shot us on sight. Plus, we know a little more about your group than you probably realize, due in part to Ms. Betty's diligence."

"Valley Hall?" Sky smiled. "Thanks for the information."

Vash frowned. "It matters little, because we are holding more cards than you think."

"So, let me get this straight," Sky said. "You three former friends of Zagan, unarmed and injured, want all of us to just walk away, so you can relocate from this...Valley Hall place...in order to make this your new stomping ground? In the hopes that you can bring Zagan's spirit...back from the dead?"

Vash smiled. "Yes, that is precisely right."

"Let me tell you what's going to happen," Sky said. "We're going to kill you, and then we're going to Valley Hall to get our boys. When we get back, we're going to burn your body in the same hole where we burned Zagan's headless corpse. Does that sound fair?"

"My dear," Vash said, "it's going to be a long day for all of us."

As Skinny Jim hovered above the men on the street from the topmost platform, he had his rifle trained on them, moving his sights from one man to the next. He couldn't make out everything they were saying, but he heard bits and pieces.

He heard Zagan's name mentioned, and his curiosity peaked. Though, he was distracted when one of the guards from the heights made his way to the top.

Skinny Jim looked over his shoulder and saw him coming. It was a man he knew in passing, but not by name.

"I got this up here," Skinny Jim said. "Maybe you should go to the third floor in case they need you. It's pretty tight quarters up here."

"I just wanted to check things out from on top," the man said as he continued to approach. "They have plenty of people down there."

He came up alongside Skinny and peered over the edge. "Christ, I hate heights."

"Then why did you come up to the tippy top of the roof?" Skinny Jim said.

The man didn't answer, so Skinny Jim lowered his rifle. The man was staring at him with a crooked grin.

As Vash implied some sinister upper hand, Skinny Jim came flying off the roof with a scream. His body hit the ground with a thud and splattered alongside Ms. Betty's corpse. The men on the street looked shocked, as if even they were taken off guard.

They looked up at the roof, and one of the heights' guards waved back.

Sky instantly retreated in the doorway and found several guns pointed in her and Baby's direction. It was three of the heights reinforcements who had taken up positions on the first floor.

"Drop them," one of the men said.

Lego, Baby, and Sky dropped their weapons.

"What is going on here?" Sky asked. "You guys are here to help *us*, not them. They're murderers. They just killed one of your own!"

"Well, we didn't expect that, either," one of the men said. "But nobody else has to get hurt. All you have to do is get the hell out, and let these guys come in. Then you can go get your friends, and *we* will return to the heights. Then you, Charlie, and all your other people can go find another place to live."

"Why?" Sky asked.

"We're just following orders," the man said. "New orders. Charlie is no longer in control of the heights."

Sky shook her head in protest.

"They think they can bring a man back from the dead," Sky said. "They're crazy. You think they'll just leave you alone? They are friends with the man who attacked your community last year!"

"You're wasting time," the man said. "Now let's just get on with this."

Sky was dumbfounded. They were weaponless and being held at gunpoint in their own home. The fortress. This was a first. Her mind raced into action.

Standing at a hallway window on the second floor, Wyatt watched the entire exchange between Sky and Vash, prepared to shoot if necessary. With the three men so exposed, the odds didn't seem too much in their favor.

Then Skinny Jim came flying off the roof, and Wyatt found himself at the wrong end of a rifle as he struggled to grasp what he had just witnessed. He liked Skinny Jim. The boy volunteered to leave the heights to come to the fortress, and this was not how anyone expected it to end for him.

Todd had stepped away from Wyatt and was pointing his weapon at his head. Though Todd seemed ill confident, it didn't take away from the seriousness of Wyatt's position.

"Drop it, Wyatt," Todd said. "I really don't want to hurt you, but I don't have a choice in this."

"There's always a choice, Todd," Wyatt said. "What are you doing? We go back like three years."

"None of it matters anymore," Todd said. "Maybe it never did. Relationships in this world...what do they really mean? It's survival. That's all that matters."

"No, it ain't, Todd," Wyatt said. "All you need to do is spend a week here to learn that lesson. Someone just threw Jim off the damn roof! Is that how you want to live?"

Wyatt shoved the barrel of the rifle away from his face, and it went off. The bullet shattered a hole in the wall behind him. He then drew his own gun and fired a single shot, which tore through Todd's upper right chest.

Todd reacted on pure adrenaline and swung the butt of his rifle. It hit Wyatt in the head and propelled him back against the hallway wall.

Todd raised his rifle again, poised to shoot, and Wyatt dove to the floor just as another bullet sounded off and ripped through the wall, sending pieces of plaster scattering. Wyatt, gun still in hand, ran down the hallway and dove into Baby's bedroom, which was across the hallway from the stairwell, as the guard from the roof, Garrity, came trampling down from the third floor.

Wyatt collected his breath as he hugged the wall beside the bedroom door with his back. He heard gunfire and mayhem on the first floor and prayed that the others were safe. The thought of what happened to Skinny Jim made him grimace.

"Where did he go?" Garrity asked as he stood on the landing to the steps.

"In that room right next to you!" Todd pointed.

Garrity turned as Wyatt, having stepped outside the room, fired a single shot from his revolver that landed between Garrity's eyes. He crumpled to the floor, and Wyatt fired off two more shots toward Todd before ducking back into the room; one hit him in the stomach and the other shattered the glass of the window behind him.

Injured, Todd moved into Misty and JZ's bedroom at the opposite end of the hall from where Wyatt was still taking cover.

"Drop it, Todd," Wyatt yelled. "You're a shitty shot. You're going to end up just like the other one."

Todd did not respond, so Wyatt peered out from the bedroom. The yelling and shooting from the first floor continued, but he didn't want to leave unfinished business on the second floor.

He noticed Todd was no longer in the hallway, so he left Baby's bedroom and carefully crept down the corridor, stepping over Garrity's fallen body to get by, realizing that Todd could pop out of one of the other rooms at any second. Slowly, he approached Misty and JZ's bedroom on his left. He turned the corner, gun pointed straight ahead, and he saw Todd's legs on the floor, sticking out from along the other side of JZ's former bed.

He carefully approached, until he saw the bloodied man over the top of the bed. His rifle was laying across his chest and he was shaking and staring off blankly. His shirt was blood-soaked and his face pale.

Damn it, Todd. Was it worth it?

Wyatt lowered his gun and grabbed the butt end of the rifle and pulled it away from him. He shook his head as Todd bled out, but then quickly turned around to address the first-floor situation.

Neck, groin, and eyes. Never play nice when trying to save your life. Hit them where they are most vulnerable.

As Sky raced to consider her options, one of the men reached behind her and made a motion to open the door to let their attackers in. As soon as eye contact shifted, she kicked him in the groin as hard as she could, and he keeled over with a yelp. She ran straight down the corridor while Leo and Baby darted in the same direction through the living room and kitchen, respectively. One of the men took a shot at them as they fled, and the bullet caught the wall near the entryway, inches away from Lego.

Lego ran down the stairs to retrieve more weapons from the arsenal while Sky opened a cabinet drawer and pulled out a revolver. She returned fire as the three men, now set up in the living room, behind the main stairs, and in the dining room, took cover.

"Dammit, girl!" he said. "You couldn't have just made this simple."

Sky heard a series of thuds and gun shots as Wyatt struggled upstairs with another of the heights' party members. Lego soon came up with more handguns. Misty grabbed one and regarded it with a distasteful expression.

"A handgun?" she said. "Surely you could have found something that would put a quicker end to this."

"And obliterate the fortress while we're at it?" Lego said.

"It wouldn't be the first time we had to rebuild from the inside out," she said as the men continued to fire shots at them, each taking turns popping out from their respective corners.

"You're going to pay for that kick, girly," the man by the stairs squealed.

"I hope Wyatt's okay," Sky said as the three hid out near the kitchen stairwell.

"Maybe I should try to cross over and get outside and come around," Lego suggested.

"Just stay put for now," Sky said. "It's too dangerous with bullets flying."

As they concluded to lie in wait under cover, they heard a voice that sounded like Charlie.

And it was. He had come to their rescue.

Eighteen

The rain stopped in the middle of the night. Miracle continued to sleep soundly under the cover of the blanket. And though Yamil had dozed off, he was too alert to feel sleepy. He worried about the bad man finding them. If he figured out that they had sneaked away, he would come looking for them, and probably check all the nearby houses. There didn't seem to be too many of them around.

He sat on the chair wondering when the right time to leave would be. It was quiet outside. The old empty house was creepy, but not as creepy as the woods at night. He watched Miracle sleep. As the rain stopped, the skies cleared and the moonlight prevailed. The open skies had become a more significant blessing after the fall because at nighttime, it was the only light available in the outside world unless there was a fire, and Yamil didn't know how to make fire. Sim had taught them in one of his lessons and had them all practice, but it was hard.

Find fire. If something is burning, take embers from it, because that is all you need.

Use glass to concentrate the sunlight on dry debris. Magnifying glasses work great, or spectacles.

Use flint with dry debris.

Sim showed them all the tricks and warehoused flint sticks as one of the many tools to create fire. He used propane with functional grills to cook meat and also to get a spark. Yamil thought about this as he remembered. Did this house have a grill?

With the extra light provided by the moon, Yamil left the couch, realizing he was still in his underwear. He felt his clothes, and though they were still damp, he put them on as he set out to locate a grill. He proceeded more confidently through the house and popped open the back door. That's where Sim kept the fortress grills, in the back. He looked and felt around in the small yard bordered by the woods. There it was, sitting on a small patch of concrete at the left side of the house.

He walked over to it and opened the lid. It didn't look to be in bad shape. It had been protected from the heavy elements by a metal overhang that extended from the house. The damp, cold air nipped at his body, and he hugged himself as he kneeled to see if there was a tank underneath.

Sure enough, the gray tank was sitting there as if waiting to be discovered. Yamil remembered seeing the grill lit many times at the fortress and tried to remember the steps.

Turn the knob.

Push the ignitor.

Turn the flames on.

He remembered the ignitor required a battery, and was worried that the battery could be dead. Batteries lasted a long time, Sim said, but it had been a long time since Sim found him.

The shelf life on batteries is many years, so we have plenty of time to figure out how to restore electricity or make more batteries. Whatever comes first.

Yamil felt around for the ignitor button. And when he pressed it, he clapped at hearing the clicking sound indicate that it was working. He knelt back down and turned the knob on the propane. And once the gas was flowing, he pressed the ignitor button and fired up the burners. The heat blasted his face, and it was the warmest he had ever felt in his life. He stood in front of the grill and watched the fire burn as he rubbed his chest and legs to facilitate the complete drying of his clothing. The heat coursed from the center of his frame out to his extremities, and he was so happy.

He ran back into the house, stubbing his toe on jagged kitchen linoleum as he soared back to Miracle's side. He stirred him awake as he grabbed his damp clothing. Miracle rubbed his eyes and sat on the edge of the couch.

"Where are my clothes?" he asked. "I'm tired."

"There's fire," Yamil said proudly. "In the back. On the grill like the fortress one."

Miracle slipped on his damp clothing, and Yamil led him to the rear of the house where the grill roared. Miracle smiled when he saw it because he felt shivery. The two continued to warm themselves and their clothes for several minutes.

"How did you do it?" Miracle asked, rubbing his hands together.

"It was a cinch," Yamil said. "I remembered."

As the boys played fireside, Yamil patted Miracle's belly through his shirt. "You have a fat belly," he laughed.

Miracle poked Yamil's belly. "You have a fat belly."

"I do not," he said. "I'm skinny."

"Watch," Yamil said as he turned around and pointed his butt at the fire. "I'm getting my butt warm."

Miracle doubled over laughing and turned around and pointed his behind at the fire. "I'm getting *my* butt warm," he laughed.

'You're a copycat," Yamil accused, lovingly so.

"*You're* a copycat," Miracle said.

That is how they spent ten minutes of their time at the grill. Warming, laughing, and relishing the moment of freedom. Not only freedom from the man who had taken them, but from everything. They were on their own, and though they longed to be back home, they savored this rare moment of independence and waywardness.

When they were sufficiently warm and revived, the moon was fading as sunrise loomed, and the pair could see well enough to hunt for more food. They found more beans, moldy green bread that was in a package that looked to have been torn apart by animals, bottled water, canned soups, two jars of peanut butter, and a box of rice.

They were no strangers to rice, as it was one of the staples at the fortress. Sim had tons of boxes and bags of rice, and they ate it almost every night. He trained them on the simplicity of making it.

"We can eat this," Yamil said. "Go find a pot."

Miracle scrambled atop a kitchen counter and retrieved a cooking pot from one of the shelves. He jumped back down with it, and Yamil poured some of the rice into the pot. He added some bottled water to it, and the pair heated it up on the grill. Once the rice soaked up the water, they ate it out of the pot with their bare hands.

With the rain stopped, their clothing dried, and their tummies full, they left the house after finding a black duffle bag to carry some other food. Yamil put the duffle bag on his back and off they went at the break of dawn, following the road but remaining in the trees that ran alongside it. They had no idea where they were going, but they did know they were looking for a big green bridge, and at least Yamil was confident that they would find it.

As they trudged through the wet foliage, Yamil stopped them when he heard a noise he couldn't discern. They ducked down in the woods, keeping an eye behind them to make sure nobody was in pursuit. He wondered what the bad man must have thought when he realized they had escaped.

The noise they were hearing was familiar, and with each passing second, it grew louder and louder, coming from the direction that they were traveling.

It was the sound of a dog barking.

Yamil immediately thought of Gigi and jumped out of the woods with Miracle behind him. The boys delighted in seeing Gigi sprinting down the road, her tongue hanging from her mouth, and they ran to her as fast as they could run. Seconds later, Gigi was in their arms, licking each of their faces. She was dirty and wet, but she was the same old Gigi.

"You found us, girl," Yamil said.

They enveloped her in their arms for several minutes, but then realized it was time to get moving again. With the reunion over, the two continued forward with their faithful companion at their sides.

"That was fun," Miracle said as they walked.

"Fun?" Yamil said. "Are you crazy? That was scary."

"Not waking up in the bad place," Miracle said. "The house."

"Yeah, that was fun," Yamil said. "I like the fire. And finding Gigi."

The road seemed long, but the pair followed it a good hour or two as the sun rose, and eventually it led them past a school. Miracle saw the swings and wanted to cross the street and visit it, but Yamil wouldn't allow it.

The bad men will see us if we are on those swings.

"Is that a school?" Miracle asked.

"I think so," Yamil said.

"I never got to go to school," Miracle said. "I know people who did."

"Yeah, goof nut," Yamil said. "So do I. Our brothers and sisters. They said learning at home at the fortress is better."

Miracle slapped is forehead. "Oh, that's right."

The pair kept on, and eventually were forced to depart the woods at an intersection. They ran quickly to the other side and ended up in the parking lot of a convenience store. The glass windows in the front were busted out and Yamil led them inside, first stopping in the front to listen for any noises. Hearing nothing, he entered with Miracle trailing behind.

"What are we doing here?" Miracle asked.

"Looking for a light," he said. "Like a flashlight. Then we can see in the dark."

It was a small store that had been ransacked. Most of the shelves were empty, toppled, or yielding inedible food. Yamil did come across a pack of batteries, so he put them in his duffle bag. It was Miracle who found the double pack of mini flashlights that were on the ground, obscured by a shelving unit. Gigi spent her time slurping up water from puddles of rain that had pooled on the floor through holes in the roof.

"I found these!" Miracle yelled. He held the pack up high and Yamil took them.

Yamil opened them up and pushed the buttons to see if the batteries came with them. They shined bright, and it was another victory for them. Yamil put the flashlights into his duffle bag and slung it across his back.

As they moved to the door, they heard a noise. It was the sounds of feet shuffling. There was someone out there. Yamil crouched down behind some machine that said ATM and pulled Miracle down with him. Yamil put his finger to his lip to shush Miracle as he listened.

Whoever it was, they were coming closer.

Nineteen

As the afternoon wore on and late evening arrived, Teddy had become more lucid and was asking for something to eat. Malayah fixed him rice and black beans, which he ate carefully while King surveyed the situation out front from the window.

"We need to start thinking about breaking out of here now that Teddy is well enough to travel," King said. "I can carry him."

"I don't need you to carry me," he said. "I can walk. I'm not dying, you know."

"You almost did," King reminded. "That'll make some hell of a days-gone-by story, that's for sure."

"What is going on out there, anyway?" Teddy asked. He was a bit out of it when things went left. "Where's Charlie?"

"We don't know," King said. "But hopefully, at the fortress by now."

King glanced out the picture window, which faced the perimeter of the community compound. Tony was standing there with five other men. There was another man lying face down on the ground where he had fallen after Charlie shot him during the earlier encounter.

Six out back and two out front. We all have weapons. No need to sit here. We can take them out easily.

"We're ready when you are, King," Frankie said. "But I'm shooting that *puta* dead after what he's done."

"You'd think he would know us well enough to know we won't just sit here while the fortress is being attacked."

"Maybe we won't have to break out," King said, peering out the window.

Malayah and Frankie appeared at his side, and they saw more than fifty residents approaching Tony from the perimeter.

Frankie pointed. "Oh, hell, it's Mrs. Chandler, and she looks mad as hell."

"I see Jordan and Bobby," Malayah pointed. "They're packing heat."

"Gordo, too!" Frankie laughed. "Oh, shit, Tony is in trouble now, thinking he had the upper hand. He thought Charlie's people were just going to sit back and let him take over? Hell no!"

"I want to see," Teddy whined from the couch.

Frankie, King, and Malayah stood proudly at the window to watch the confrontation go down.

After leaving her dental apartment, Mrs. Chandler did not return home for the afternoon. She went building to building alerting the residents of what was happening, and she didn't hold any details back when she told the tale to the others.

Tony and some of the men he coerced from the heights militia are trying to overthrow Charlie. They killed Scooter and they have Malayah, Frankie, and a couple of our fortress allies held hostage in my apartment. We have to act quickly, or we will all be in trouble, and more people will die.

Tony did what?

Where is Charlie?

They killed Scooter? You're kidding!

Tony better not have hurt Charlie, or we'll tear him and anyone who's with him to pieces.

Where did this come from?

I thought I heard the gunshots.

Where are they?

Let's get these sons of bitches and show them who's really in charge.

The response was music to Mrs. Chandler's ears. Charlie had his weaknesses, but Mrs. Chandler knew that *he* was the heights. Since the beginning, he had shed blood, sweat, and tears in partnership with Sim and the fortress to grow a sustainable community, which had tripled in size and was now flourishing. Mrs. Chandler remembered fondly the day she met Charlie.

She found the heights on a blustery winter's day, when she thought she might freeze if she didn't find adequate shelter. Jacob, a perimeter guard, brought her straight to Charlie for emergency entry. He took her into his own apartment, wrapped her in a warm blanket, gave her tea, soup, and let her stay the night. The two chatted all night long while the snow fell outside. That's when he learned she was a dental hygienist. The next day, he provided her with an apartment, and soon after, an office to conduct dental work. He checked in on her all the time, as he did many of the residents, and nurtured connections that ultimately built a sound community.

There was no way that Tony was going to commandeer the heights with only a handful of men and some random weaponry.

Mrs. Chandler marched at the head of the group of the seventy-five people she had gathered to surround Tony. He saw them coming, and though it was unclear what he was thinking, panic was written on his face.

The group stopped about twenty yards from the men that were hovering outside of the dental apartment where King and the others were holed up. Within a minute, the other two men from around front also showed up and looked astonished at the mob that had assembled on the lawn.

"We got this under control, everyone," Tony said. "Return to your apartments. This will all be over soon, and me and my men will arrange a meeting in the community room to go over the details with everyone about the new leadership."

"New leadership?" a woman screamed. "What the hell dumb shit you talking, Tony? Where's Charlie?"

"Charlie left," Tony said. "Ran, in fact. After shooting one of our own." He pointed to the fallen guard nearby. "He put us in charge, and we are just resolving some issues we're having with a couple of our own residents and a couple of residents of the fortress. I told you, it's all under control."

"Mrs. Chandler told us everything, you fool," a man shouted from the crowd. "You killed Scooter. Scooter wouldn't have hurt a fly. You better drop them weapons, because this charade is over!"

"There's a couple of young boys inside with Malayah and Frankie," Mrs. Chandler said. "One of the boys is sick. He almost died. These men are keeping them from leaving to get to their friends. Charlie ran to the fortress to try to stop Tony's men from a coup there as well. They're trying to take over everything."

"Now, wait a minute," Tony pleaded. "You don't have all the facts here. They killed our man. Charlie is not who you—"

A shot rang out from the mob and tore through Tony's chest. He moaned and then took two steps forward before collapsing. The other men exchanged looks, then threw their guns down and started running. The mob roared and all broke into a sprint at once while Mrs. Chandler remained, facing the window. She offered a thumbs up sign as the mob brutally attacked and subdued the other men.

Back in the apartment, they were celebrating. They were so proud of the community for sticking up for Charlie, their rights, peace, and posterity.

As the mob attacked, the other insurgents were either killed or subdued, and King moved back to Teddy on the couch.

"I'm going to carry you, big man," King said. "And don't freaking argue with me. I do not want you overexerting yourself. But we got to go now."

"I'm ready, King," Teddy said.

"We're going with you," Malayah said.

"Hell yeah," Frankie agreed.

King leaned down, and Malayah helped Teddy onto King's back. She wrapped the blanket around him, and the two headed for the door. The four departed the apartment building and met up with Mrs. Chandler.

"That was amazing," King said. "We owe you everything."

"You don't owe me anything," Mrs. Chandler said. "There was no way in hell this community was allowing this. I already spoke to many of the people. I have about thirty of them going back with you right now. We're going to appoint new members to the security team right away to cover our perimeter, but you all need to get down to the fortress now and make sure Charlie and your people have the support they need. I hope it's not too late."

"It won't be," King said. "We will get there as fast as we can."

Mrs. Chandler yelled to the mob, "They're leaving! Those going to the fortress, arm yourselves quickly and meet these people on the western road. Now!"

King never observed Mrs. Chandler's authoritarian side. She seemed so meek and mild when tending to Teddy, and really any other time he had seen her. This was a side of her that was quite new. King exchanged smiles with her, and they all took off for the road.

Twenty

CHARLIE MOVED CAUTIOUSLY THROUGH the wooded area that ran parallel to the road as he made his way to the fortress. When he was close enough, he could see three men standing in the middle of the road beside two bodies. He couldn't tell whose bodies he was seeing, but it was a grim sight.

As he approached, he slowed his step. He heard gunshots from inside the fortress and his heart raced, thinking about Wyatt and the kids. Once he realized that the men out front were not his people, he stepped from the trees and made his presence known.

"Hey!" he yelled, pointing his gun at them.

The men, not expecting Charlie's intrusion, raised their hands.

"I'll shoot you dead if you give me reason," Charlie said.

Charlie approached them as he vied to get a look at the bodies on the street. The first one he saw was an older woman who was wearing a dress and looked to have a gun wound in the center of her forehead. The other body he saw was Skinny Jim. Charlie's heart sank. He looked from the body up to the roof and frothed with anger.

"Who did this?" He pointed at Vash. "Who?"

"Whoever you are, we aren't the bad guys," Vash answered. "We simply offered a proposition to the residents, but unfortunately tensions escalated, and next thing we knew, this poor gentleman was flying off the roof."

"They killed one of ours," Balaam said dispassionately.

Charlie instantly shot Balaam in the face, and he dropped to the ground alongside Ms. Betty.

"That's for JZ," he said as the other two ran off down the street.

Charlie fired off two more shots as the men zigzagged down the road and eventually darted into the yards of neighboring houses.

"Shit," he muttered to himself.

He gave Skinny Jim another glance and then ran up the fortress steps. The door was closed, but it wasn't locked. He opened it up and dove to his right side into the dining room and took cover behind a bureau that he pushed out from the wall. One of his former residents, a heights guard, was taking cover behind the main stairwell as he exchanged fire with other parties who were in the kitchen.

The man looked back over his shoulder and saw that Charlie had entered.

"Charlie?" the man said. "What the hell?"

"Screw you, Matthew," Charlie said as he popped off a shot, which ricocheted off the wooden banister.

"Hey," Matthew said. "Are you crazy?"

Charlie was trying to be mindful of how many bullets he had left in his gun.

"You're asking *me* that, you traitor?" Charlie said.

"This is all messed up, Charlie," Matthew said. "I didn't plan it this way."

"Then drop your gun and get the hell out of here," Charlie said.

Matthew considered this as he regarded the open doors at the front of the fortress. He threw down his weapon and ran out as fast as he could.

"That you, Charlie?" Wyatt called from the second floor.

"I'm here, Wyatt," Charlie said.

"Two more left somewhere," Wyatt said.

"Sky?" Charlie called. "Kids?"

"Shut up, Charlie. This our show," called another voice from the living room. "You've been ousted. Didn't Tony tell you?"

"Tony's a fool if he thinks my people are going to let this fly," Charlie said. "You all better cast those guns aside and get to running, or you're going to die right here tonight."

"Charlie?" Sky cried.

"Sky!" Charlie cried. "Is everyone all right?"

"For now," she said. "Can you handle these idiots so we can go get Yamil and Miracle?"

"You better shut up, little girl," one of the men said. Charlie saw him behind a curio cabinet on the other side of the living room.

"I see you, Trevor," Charlie said.

Charlie aimed his gun at the meat of Trevor's thigh, which was jutting out from behind the cabinet. He fired one shot, and it blew a hole in his leg.

"Ow!" Trevor cried as he collapsed onto the floor. Charlie ran over and kicked his gun away from him. The final guy lurked on the other side of the hallway.

"It's just you, Clarence," Charlie said. "You can run out that front door now or die."

"You shot, Trevor?" Clarence asked.

"He'll live," Charlie said. "For now."

Trevor was yelling as blood spurted across the dining room floor. "I need a torniquet!"

"If I run, you better not shoot me in the back," Clarence yelled.

"Nobody is shooting you in the back," Charlie said. "Though we should, for what you did to Skinny Jim."

"That wasn't me, dammit!" Clarence yelled. "That was Garrity. You know that son of a bitch is crazy."

"This move of yours isn't exactly proving *your* sanity either," Charlie said.

"Blame Tony," Clarence said. "He was the one talking about taking over and helping that guy take the fortress."

"What are you going to do, Clarence?" Charlie asked.

"I'm going!" he yelled back.

Clarence bolted from the living room to the front door. As he made it to the threshold, Wyatt fired from the main stairwell and the bullet struck Clarence in the back. He did a header down the fortress steps and rolled out onto the sidewalk. Wyatt walked to the doorway and observed the man's lifeless body at the bottom of the steps. He closed the doors behind him.

Wyatt walked back in and fired a bullet into Trevor's head as he worked to stop the bleeding in his thigh. Charlie shuddered.

"Sorry," Wyatt said. "You didn't hear Skinny Jim when they tossed him off that roof, though," he said.

"I'm not judging you," Charlie said. "The entire situation is absurd."

"You can come out, kids," Charlie said. "It's safe."

Leo, Misty, and Sky emerged from the kitchen. Sky and Charlie hugged as the smoke cleared.

"I'm so glad you're okay," Charlie said. "I shot one of the men that killed JZ. The other two ran off."

Sky pushed away from him. "What happened?"

"It would seem as if my trusted militia coordinator, Tony, organized a coup to take over the heights and help these other men oust you all from the fortress. I got away, but I don't know where things stand with the heights. Tony was trying to sequester us in one of the buildings, but I managed to get out of there after a fire fight."

"Well, we have to get to Valley Hall now," Sky said. "Those other two men are probably headed back there. They'll kill the boys after this!"

"I'll go too," Baby said.

"Where is Valley Hall, anyway?" Sky asked. "I'm not from around here."

"I'll lead the way," said Charlie. "I know right where it is. But Wyatt, you'll have to return to the heights and rally support. It's crazy up there right now."

"I'm on it," Wyatt pronounced.

"That leaves me and you to hold down the fort," Leo said, putting a hand on Misty's shoulder.

"And we have a lot to do, cleaning up this mess," she said.

"We should also bring up more artillery from the basement," Leo said. "Just in case we have more visitors."

Sky and Baby grabbed some weapons and their side bags, which they loaded with extra cartridges, energy bars, ponchos, and grenades. They headed for the door where Charlie was waiting.

"You better hurry," Leo said. "Bring them back safe. And look for Gigi, too."

From the sidewalk, Sky flipped Kellogg's lucky coin into the air and caught it before placing it into her pocket. She then offered Leo and Misty a long gaze. And though she said not a word, she didn't need to, because Leo heard her loud and clear. They had been out on missions plenty of times. They had gone several more miles further than on previous trips. But now they were headed toward the devil's den, and there was much at stake.

Twenty-One

As Yamil and Miracle ducked behind the ATM in the store, they heard the footsteps in the puddles outside getting closer. Yamil felt for the knife in his sock. He readied it, as it was his and Miracle's only defense.

Suddenly, the footsteps stopped. Yamil dared not look out.

"Hello?" came a voice.

Yamil looked at Miracle. Gigi must have sensed their stress because she launched into a fury. She ran out of the store barking. Miracle and Yamil stood from their crouch. They saw a young girl, perhaps in her teenage years, scrappy, with long curly hair and armed with a small gun that she had in one hand, but not aimed. Her features were soft and her eyes wide. She stepped away from Gigi with a look of panic on her face.

Gigi's bark simmered to a growl as the boys emerged.

"Please," she said. "Call her off."

"No," Yamil said, keeping Miracle behind him. "What do you want?"

She shook her head. "I only saw you...from a distance. I just...was curious."

Yamil thought about her answer, then said, "We have to go to the green bridge."

"That's not too far," the girl said. "You got lost?"

"A bad man took us," Yamil said. "He could find us. We want to go home."

Miracle peered out from behind Yamil.

"You're very young," she observed. "I don't see too many kids as young as you guys. Your home is near the green bridge?"

"Yes," Yamil said.

Gigi sat back on her hind legs, watching, but more confident.

"Gigi knows if you're bad," Miracle said from behind Yamil.

"So, what is she saying?" the girl asked.

"She would be mad if you were bad," Yamil said.

"That rhymes." The girl giggled. "I can take you back, if you want. I have people too, but they won't look for me."

Gigi stepped closer to the girl, and the girl held out her hand for Gigi to smell. Gigi sniffed her, and then sat back on her hind legs and panted. The boys smiled.

"Where do you live?" Yamil asked.

"That's for another time," she said. "I'd take you there, but it would probably scare you, since we just met. It's not really where I live...it's how I live. Yeah, that's the best way to describe it."

"Okay, then," Yamil said. "Let's go."

The girl nodded and led them away from the store and through the intersection. The road ascended, and she continued at a fast clip. Miracle was falling behind, so Yamil had to call to her to slow down. She waited for them to catch up each time.

"My feet hurt," Miracle complained. "How long till we're home?"

"Probably a long time," Yamil said. "Be brave and strong."

"It'll be a few hours of walking, for sure," the girl said. "Especially at this speed. I'm not used to traveling with people whose legs are so short." She giggled. "By the way, I'm Harlow."

"I'm Yamil. This whiny goofball is Miracle."

"Hey," Miracle whined.

"So, you say a bad man took you?" Harlow asked.

"Yeah, he was mean," Yamil said. "He was nice at first and said he would bring us to Sim, but then he put a cloth over our eyes and tied us up. It was scary."

"Real scary," Miracle said.

"I think he hurt JZ, too," Yamil said. "He was going to hurt us, but we got away with my knife and jumped out a window."

"It was cold and rainy, but we had rice and got fire on the grill," Miracle added.

"Whoa, slow down," Harlow said. "This is a lot. Who are Sim and JZ? Are these your family members?"

"They love us," Yamil said. "But they're gone. Sim taught us how to get away from bad people and how to be strong."

"I guess it worked," Harlow said.

Harlow led them past a construction company, a cornfield, and then a church that was made of brick and resembled the fortress. It had a baseball field on the side, and a pond beyond that. After the church was another intersection.

Harlow stopped at the intersection and tucked her gun into her waist. She put her hands on her hips. "Well, boys, the good news is, there are only two more roads left to travel before you're home. The bad news is, each road is very long. We'll keep at it, and if you need to stop, let me know. But the fewer breaks we take, the faster we will get there."

Yamil's feet were sore, and he knew it would be a long haul, but he didn't want to stop too much. He wanted to get back home. Sky and the others were probably worried about them. Plus, Ms. Betty was bad, and he had to tell everyone what she said and how she tricked them to go with the bad man. She might be tricking other people too.

Harlow adjusted her usual pace for the boys as they journeyed down the first of two long remaining roads home.

For Yamil and Miracle, their journey was like seeing the world for the first time. They were so little when the world died, and they couldn't remember much of anything about what it had been like before, and Sim never did let them stray from the house, go on missions, or even take them anywhere outside the creek. They had no idea what was out there until now.

When you're older.

He did walk them to the bottom of the hill to the intersection to see the turnoff to the bridge; the straight lane that led to the row houses, steel factory, and prison; and the steep hill that, if taken straight to the top, led to the point well beyond the rear of the fortress. There was a city college there where Sim and the other orphans would often go to scavenge from.

The boys did see the whole city from the rooftop a few times, but everything was so tiny from there that it was impossible to recognize anything once in the middle of it. Except for the river. Yamil figured if he couldn't get help finding the bridge that they could always look for the river and follow it until they ran into the green bridge.

They walked another thirty minutes taking in the sights. They passed more houses, stores, an ice cream stand, a car lot, banks, and many other places from the old world.

"I remember that!" Miracle pointed when he saw the golden arches of McDonald's. "That was good. Chicken nuggets."

"What's that?" Yamil asked.

"These little things," Miracle said. "They were brown and crunchy. Mommy got me sauce with them. There was french fries too."

"Oh," Yamil said. "I want some french fries."

The boys had french fries before. Sim made them himself with the potatoes he grew. Sliced them real thin, then fried them up in oil. The boys loved them, but Sim didn't make them too much. He said they weren't healthy.

"Yeah, that's the worst part of this crappy world," Harlow said. "You guys probably didn't know too much before it ended, and that's probably better. You don't know what you're missing. Malls, movies, smartphones...even school. I complained back then, but what I wouldn't give to be back at school right now with all my friends. Not one of them made it."

"My mom died," Miracle said.

"Mine too," Yamil added.

"Everyone's did," Harlow said solemnly.

As the boys continued to be mesmerized by new places, Gigi kept alongside them, stopping occasionally to sniff the ground or go to the bathroom. As they made their way down the road, they came across a plaza with old stores and other businesses, all shuttered. As Yamil was observing the scene, he saw words that caught his attention.

"Wait a minute," he said.

Cut Above the Rest Nail and Hair Salon.

He remembered the shirt JZ used to wear with the emblem on it. He smiled large. "That's JZ."

Yamil ran toward the store with Gigi on his heels. Harlow was confused, but she took Miracle's hand and the two ran after Yamil to see what had excited him. Yamil ran into the plaza parking lot and stopped in front of the store.

"What is it?" Harlow asked as she and Miracle caught up with him.

"I remember the story," Yamil said, staring through the glass. "This is where Sim found her."

"There are a lot of hair salons out there, Yamil," Harlow said. "It may not be the right one."

"It is!" he said pointing up at the sign. "That's the sign."

"Okay, then," Harlow said.

Yamil pulled open the glass door with some effort and wandered in. Everything was dusty and dirty. It was quiet. He saw a bunch of chairs sitting in front of glass mirrors and went and stood in front of one. He looked at himself. There were mirrors at the fortress, but not mirrors like this. He brushed back his hair and smiled at himself.

Miracle and Harlow stood alongside him, each regarding themselves in the mirror.

"Wow," Harlow said. "I probably haven't seen myself in a month. I wish there was someone working, because I need a damn haircut."

Yamil laughed. Then he saw something else that drew his attention. It was a picture taped to the mirror in front of one of the chairs. It was JZ and some lady. He reached out and pulled it down.

"That's JZ," Miracle said.

"Yeah," Yamil said, remembering the last time he saw her at dinner. He felt sad.

"That's your friend?" Harlow asked.

"That's JZ," Yamil said. "Sim was here."

Yamil looked around as he thought about the day Sim had described to them, when he entered the store and sat down and JZ gave him a haircut. He looked at the floor, and he wondered if all the hair on the floor surrounding the chair was Sim's. Who's else would it be? He reached down and picked some loose strands up and dropped them again.

Sim, he thought.

"Can we go now?" Miracle asked.

"Okay," Yamil said, after placing the picture into his bag. "Everyone will be happy to see the picture."

After leaving the hair and nail salon, they continued on the road.

Twenty-Two

When Charlie, Sky, and Baby made it to the intersection downhill from the fortress, they regarded the clouds that were forming and hoped they weren't an omen. There was little chance that they would catch up to Vash and the other guy, so Sky's only hope was that they continued to hold the boys as bargaining chips instead of hurting them. She couldn't lose them. She had taken care of those boys since they were three years old. She taught them to read and speak. She tucked them in every night. She sang to them. She held their hands and protected them. They were her loves.

Throughout the ordeal of them going missing, she tried to remain objective about the situation, as so many had been lost before this, including JZ, so she understood that being realistic about life and death in these days was essential. But still, she couldn't help but feel haunted by the thought of Yamil and Miracle being gone, and being on the road and away from all the circumstances that held her attention made it easier to dwell upon.

They were only a quarter mile along the way when Baby heard Sky sniffling. It was clear that she was crying, and this was rare for Sky, but she understood. Charlie turned around and noticed her emotion as well.

"It'll be okay, Sky," Charlie said, pulling out a flask from his coat and taking a swig. "No matter what, it'll be okay."

Sky didn't acknowledge his remarks. She only needed a moment. She would write about all her feelings another time. The first couple of entries she added to her book helped her cope. She understood why Sim journaled. It might not have been for the future generations to read, or for the orphans to learn more about him. He might have only been doing it as a form of release. To write down the things he couldn't say. To convey his emotions so he didn't have to carry them on his shoulders or express them out loud to the others.

As they continued their walk, her thoughts shifted to her Uncle Mike, always on her mind post-Sim. Maybe it was her new sense of need for a fatherly figure since Sim died, or maybe it was a new maturity that resurrected this yearning to find out what happened to him. She so deeply wanted to know if he was alive or dead. Yet, she realized, but had not yet reconciled, that she likely would never have those answers.

Uncle Mike was her rock before the fall, and even after. Her mother and father were strongly religious, and they raised Sky with those values. Though their intentions were good, they were very strict parents, and as she got a little older, it interfered with her social life. It was her Uncle Mike who convinced her parents to let her go to a junior high dance, let her watch certain R-rated movies, and let her skip church on occasion for school functions. He helped her to escape and live more like other kids. But above and beyond that, he was strong and protective. He had no kids of his own, so she was his surrogate.

Sky shook her head as she tried to stifle her tears. She would never have figured that love would be the biggest problem of all in these times. Like a double-edged sword, it cut both ways. It made one strong *and* weak.

"We're going to find them," Baby said.

But will they still be alive when we do? Sky wondered.

"I know they'll be there," Baby continued. "We'll rescue them and bring them home."

Charlie remained quiet. Sky knew he loved them too. Perhaps not in the same way as her, but in his own way. Sky didn't need Charlie to tell her how angry he was or how worried he was for the boys' safety. She knew.

"This world," Sky said. "It makes you wonder all the time."

"The old world did too," Charlie said. "You weren't around long enough to know, Sky, but the old world made you wonder all the time. About life, death, people, fate. In truth, this world isn't too much different from the old one. It's just quieter...most of the time."

"It's not about the world being good or bad, I guess," Sky contended. "Just figuring out how to rise above it all, despite the challenges."

"Maybe if we just solve one problem at a time, we can work everything out and make things the way they need to be," Charlie said. "Didn't you ever hear that expression 'Rome wasn't built in a day'?"

"I suppose," Sky said.

"Sim gave us a good start, though," Baby said.

"That he did," Charlie said.

Charlie led them up a hill beyond the intersection, and after a mile of walking, cut over onto a side street. Baby and Sky had been down that road many times scouring neighborhood houses for supplies. As the sidewalk welcomed what was once a busy road, they saw a corner store, and on the other side of the road, the large black gates that surrounded the perimeter of Emma Willard School. The girls' school campus was sprawling, and on the west side there were big hills that Sim brought them to occasionally during winter so they could sleigh ride. There was also a huge gymnasium where King, Ace, and Shark played basketball while the younger children pulled out mats to do gymnastics. They even had a horse that Flip used to practice his acrobatics.

Days gone by.

"How far away is this, anyway, Charlie?" Baby said.

"I thought you'd never ask," Charlie said, keeping a brisk pace. "In total, a few miles. It'll just feel like more because we're all worried."

"Should we expect only three of them?" Sky asked.

"Who knows," Charlie said. "I see they had a woman in their group. I got one of them, but the other two ran. There would be at least one guarding the boys...they got to my heights people. God knows what we'll be facing up there. I can tell you the place is no fortress. It's a shithole. The home was closed and abandoned years before the fall. What purpose it serves for them, I'll never know."

Sky said, "Ms. Betty mentioned bringing Zagan back from the dead. Zagan always felt he was doing the devil's work. Now we know why."

"A Satanic cult?" Charlie said.

"Zagan went rogue," Sky said. "They just caught up with him."

"They're all deranged," Charlie said. "It's dangerous to make assumptions, but how many Satan worshippers could possibly be left in the world? From what we have seen so far, it sounds more like this army is nothing more than a handful of fanatics."

The group passed a cemetery, crossed a small bridge over a gorge where Sim had a few times taken them swimming, and then made a right at a gas station that was just past the bridge.

"Two more roads," Charlie said.

"Thanks for leading the way, Charlie," Sky said, "when your own people are in trouble."

"You are *all* my people," Charlie said. "And Wyatt will handle it. And you know King won't remain idle while they try to keep him away from you. Sometimes, Sky, you have to realize you can't handle everything by yourself. We alone aren't the fortress. Our people are just as passionate and capable as us, and their resilience is as strong as our own. Have faith."

They passed several homes before houses became sparse, while open land and cornfields became more prominent. They passed a baseball field and a community library before finally reaching another intersection where there was a ramshackle convenience store.

A half mile down a straight road, they came across a windy side road that ascended steeply. Charlie stopped them there.

Redemption Road.

"It's at the top of this road," Charlie said. "Are you ready to get these boys back?"

Sky didn't answer. She simply took the lead up the hill.

Twenty-Three

After Charlie, Sky, and Baby left the fortress, Leo visited the arsenal and brought up some more guns, including semi-automatics, knives, and pistols. He then raced around the first floor of the fortress. He started at the front of the house. Then he checked the east and west sides. Finally, he checked the back yard from the kitchen window. He wanted to keep a close eye on the perimeter. All seemed quiet, so he returned to the first floor to help Misty pull the bodies into a heap at the kitchen door.

They worked upward in the house collecting the dead. The two dragged the man named Trevor to the door, leaving a trail of blood through the house, before going upstairs and, one at a time, dragging the bodies of the other two men by their legs down the back steps into the kitchen.

The pair was covered with blood and panting heavily by the time they got the corpses ready to be put outside.

"What about the bodies out front?" Leo asked, eyeing the carnage on the street from the window as the sun began to dip in the sky.

"It's too much, right now," Misty said. "I'm dying, here. Plus, we can't be exposed out there for that long. Let's just quickly put these bodies on the porch so we can get to monitoring."

"We can leave the bodies for now," Leo suggested, "and deal with it later."

"It won't take long," Misty said. "I don't want to be in this house with a bunch of dead bodies lying around," Misty protested.

"Then let's get them out of here and be done with it," Leo said.

Misty opened the door, and she and Leo moved the bodies out one at a time, leaving a pool of blood in front of the door. After they had gotten the third body out onto the deck, they went to close the door and Vash and Amon burst in.

Leo and Misty tried to reach fast for their weapons, but the men had surprised them. Vash and Amon were on them quickly, and each of the adults landed a solid punch to each child's face in unison. Misty and Leo were thrust to the ground on impact, and as they were dazed and confused, they were at the whim of the madmen.

After Charlie shot Balaam, Vash and Amon had fled as bullets whizzed over their heads. Charlie headed into the fortress, while Vash and Amon fell back nearby. They circled back around, approaching the fortress from the rear. They did not fear being spotted, as they knew the roof guard had been eliminated.

Though they knew Charlie had not given chase and instead chose to enter the fortress, they had no way to know the position of the heights militia men who were holding things down in the fortress.

The pair took up behind the fortress wall, not too far from where Pan had enticed Yamil and Miracle to follow him from the compound. They heard faint noises and gunfire coming from the fortress but had no context.

"Balaam," Amon said. The men had been friends for years.

Vash put a hand on Amon's shoulder. "It was unexpected."

"What are we doing?" Amon asked. "We should go back and retrieve those little ones and cut their throats right in front of their loved ones for what they've done."

"They're in good hands with Pan," Vash said. "Let's see how things go here, first. Just because Balaam is gone, does not mean our plan has failed. We still have men inside."

"What was this all for?" Amon asked. "Bringing Zagan back, even if it ends up killing the rest of us?"

"Because Zagan isn't like the rest of us," Vash said. "If we die in returning him, then the sacrifice will be worth it."

They kept a close eye on the fortress from the wall, in time venturing for a closer view. They moved their position to the well, then the outhouse, still wondering if the men inside had subdued their foes.

"I'm going back around to observe," Amon asked. "If the men have control of the fortress, they'll be looking for us there."

Amon skirted around the fortress, and Vash lost sight of him.

As he waited for him to return, Vash noted the bouquet of flowers where Sim had fallen. There were pictures and other mementos left there as well.

That's where Zagan took down their leader.

Ave Satanas.

He waited another thirty minutes by the outhouse building until Amon returned, undetected.

"What did you see?" Vash asked.

"It's not good," Amon said. "They managed to get the best of those people from the heights. One of them is out on the street, dead."

"Peculiar with the element of surprise how they could mess that up," Vash said.

"That man who shot Balaam left with two of the others, probably for Valley Hall. That means there can't be more than a couple of them left inside. If we can somehow get in, we can subdue them easily. They're just children, after all."

"Children," Vash said. "We've underestimated them time and again. Children, perhaps, but not children like in the old world. A warrior is a warrior, no matter what the age."

"It's the best chance we have," Amon said. "Unless we go back and get the other two of their friends."

Just as he said this, the door to the deck off the kitchen opened, and they saw a girl and a boy moving bodies out to the porch.

"Maybe our luck has changed," Vash said.

Amon redirected his gaze upon the fortress porch and smiled.

This was their chance.

After Misty and Leo had been felled, Amon ran to the basement looking for cord or rope so he could properly restrain them. He saw their indoor garden, their arsenal, which Leo had failed to lock after he seized more weapons from it, and he unlocked the door to the underground passage.

Ultimately, he discovered zip ties and ran them upstairs. They bound Misty and Leo's hands behind their backs as they lay on the floor in a daze.

"Now what?" Amon said.

Vash put a finger over his lips and listened. He wasn't sure if there was anyone else in the house. They quietly sneaked around the first floor, then the second, and finally the third until they were comfortable that only Leo and Misty had remained.

The first and second floors were stained with blood and littered with pieces of glass and plaster. Once Vash realized they had authority over the fortress, he threw out his arms.

"We're here!" he yelled. "Zagan, we did it."

When he returned to the kitchen, Misty and Leo were looking at them, defiantly.

"You haven't accomplished anything that Zagan hadn't accomplished himself," Misty said, her lip fat and bloody, and the white of one eye reddened from ruptured blood vessels.

"What are you talking about?" Vash said.

"Zagan made it in," she said, wincing in pain. "We killed him in the living room. We hacked him to bits and shot him in the head."

Vash stared into the kitchen ceiling. "It would explain why I feel his energy in here. It's overpowering. He's still here. Waiting."

"That's Sim you feel," Leo said. "He's the biggest spirit in this place."

"We will see," Vash said.

Twenty-Four

Sky led the way up Redemption Road. The road spiraled up and around in between two sets of tall trees that loomed over them ominously.

Nobody talked as they hiked the pathway to the top.

Charlie was trying to fathom how they were going to devise an invasion of the lair, trying to remember what the place looked like. One of his former Grizzland Heights buddies was placed there back in the day, and Charlie had visited him on a couple of occasions. It was a modest-sized building, he recalled, almost like a regular house where teens had to live when they broke the law or were taken out of their regular homes.

Baby wondered how many people might be defending the home, thinking about the fortress and how it was secured. If they had fortified Valley Hall in such a way, it would be impossible for them to get at the boys.

Sky was only thinking about Yamil and Miracle. Were they alive or dead? Tied up? Placed into a locked room? Did they have food? Were they being tortured and maimed like JZ had been?

It was dusk by the time they made it to the top. The clouds were releasing a drizzle, as well, and Valley Hall looked like a haunted house, cast in the shadow of the descending sun, lit from inside with a few small lights assumed to be lanterns.

Here we go.

The building had two stories, white-sided and spray painted with graffiti. It had a main entrance and a side entrance. Its windows were mostly all boarded up, which meant nobody would be watching their approach. It had a circular driveway out front that was overgrown with weeds. It was surrounded by trees on all sides. There was a patch of overgrown grass in the middle of the driveway boasting a broken sign that was hanging from a single rusted chain.

Welcome to Valley Hall.

"That's where they are," Baby said. "What do we do?" she asked, clutching her M-16.

"Let's go by the side entrance, instead of through the front doors," Charlie said. "This old place is going to make a lot of noise, so tread carefully."

Together, they crept toward the two-story home, proceeding toward the left side entrance from the right so that they did not have to cross in front of the building. They wandered down a stamped concrete pathway that had eroded over time to the back side of the house, staying close to the building until they came around on the left where the secondary entrance was located.

"This place isn't that big so there aren't going to be too many places to hide," Baby warned.

"Ironic that these people should want to move from an orphanage of the past to an orphanage of the new world," Charlie said.

"I can see why," Sky said. "Look at this place."

"Keep in mind," Charlie said, "the fortress and the heights may not look too much different now, if they had not been maintained. These bastards simply want what they didn't have the wherewithal to create."

"I guess in their minds it's easier to take, than make," Sky said.

Through the left door, they entered the home cautiously. The door swung open without the dramatics of endless slow creaking, and they realized they were at the top of a wooden stairway that ascended one way or descended the other.

Sky removed a flashlight from her bag, and before turning it on, she whispered to Baby. "Be ready to fire at anyone that isn't Yamil or Miracle."

She shone the flashlight down the set of collapsing blue stairs and took Baby and Charlie downward. They entered a large room below ground level that was full of debris. It was an open space with wooden floors that looked like it may have been some sort of gymnasium in its time. Sky zoomed the flashlight around the room and noticed another empty room that may have been an office or storage.

As they explored the vast nothingness of the underground room, they heard footsteps above them that came in a series of creaking noises. Sky turned off her flashlight and they listened.

The pacing increased. Back and forth. Back and forth. Then those footsteps got closer to the stairwell that they had just descended. The person clomped down the stairs from the first floor to the landing. But instead of rounding the stairs into the subfloor where they were, he opened the door they had just entered, and it slammed shut behind him.

Once they could no longer hear the steps above them, they raced for the stairs leading to the exit. Sky kept her flashlight off and the three of them felt their way around without the benefit of having a visual path. Halfway up the dilapidated set of stairs, the door flung open again and whoever entered cursed.

Damn.

What is he mad about? Sky wondered.

She swallowed hard as she saw the beam of a flashlight flickering around a few feet away. The light shone in their direction and froze on them. Baby couldn't see who was behind it, as she was blinded by the beam of light, but *he* surely saw them standing there.

"Hey!" he yelled.

Baby stepped out from behind Charlie and Sky and squeezed the trigger of her M-16. The man immediately ducked as a hail of bullets sprayed the stairwell, door, and wall of the small entryway foyer. Sky charged upstairs while withdrawing a revolver from her side bag. She hurriedly flipped her flashlight back on as she reached the doorway. Baby and Charlie arrived behind her and they all listened.

"So much for the element of surprise," Baby said.

"Keep going," Charlie yelled. "We're boxed in down here."

"We have to move fast!" Sky yelled.

Sky moved briskly up the stairs to the first level with Baby and Charlie right behind. She shone the light into a bathroom space. They ducked in and she quickly surveyed the space, moving past a couple of sinks, one of which was falling off the wall, to a second part that had a tub and shower area. Seeing nothing, she headed back toward the door where Baby stood, peering out into the corridor with her own flashlight.

"What if we're walking into a trap?" Baby whispered.

"Just stay low and be ready to fire," Sky said, breezing past her into the hall.

Sky took them down a corridor, which was a balcony overlooking the gym below. It led to another, larger room, which was lightly furnished with a couple of old chairs and some mattresses strewn on the floor with blankets. There was nowhere to duck and cover, should they have to, and it made Sky feel vulnerable.

Off to her left was a kitchen, and they quickly veered off into it. It was a relic of the past, but offered them more cover should someone go on the offensive. Sky wondered how many people were in the house and what they might be up to. They could no longer hear footsteps, nor did they hear anyone leave, so whomever they had encountered was still in the home, probably waiting for them.

As they made their way through the home, following the path of the flashlight, Charlie recalled the days of his visit. He was in awe of what it looked like compared to how he remembered it.

They made their way through the large kitchen, crunching on glass as they walked past a spot where there used to be a stove but now only had an electrical outlet post sticking out of the broken tiled floor. There were several empty cabinets and cupboards with doors sprung open, revealing nothing but empty space. The countertops were littered with shards of wood and glass, as well as beer and soda cans from squatters.

They arrived at a second part of the kitchen which looked out into another room through serving windows, most likely where the residents picked up their meal from the kitchen.

That's when the first spray of ammunition from the offense shattered the stillness. They all took cover underneath the serving windows as random gunfire continued for ten more seconds, splitting wood cabinetry and exploding the plaster walls around and beyond them.

The girls turned off their flashlights and waited as the gunfire ceased. Sky could hear Baby breathing heavily and worried about her having a panic attack. She had come a long way since the days of Zagan and had worked on the relaxation techniques Sim had taught her almost every day. She hadn't had a panic attack in several weeks, but when she did, it required time and patience to help her through it.

Sky put a reassuring hand on her knee and squeezed it gently. She feared offering words that would give their position away.

"So, you found us," a cryptic voice spoke. "You know what they say about the best laid plans."

Sky realized with those comments, that this man must not have spoken to the others that fled the fortress. What did that mean? Did they somehow beat them back to Valley Hall, or did they not come back at all, meaning they were still at the fortress?

"Give us our boys," Sky dared. "Your plan is ruined. Your men have run away like cowards. It's over."

"It's not over until the devil says," the man answered.

"God has said," Sky returned. "And that's enough."

"So you think," the voice said.

"Where are they?" Sky said, wanting to be strong, but realizing her voice was trembling. "I want to hear them."

"They are with me," the voice said. "And they will be sacrificed, like the rest of you."

"I don't believe you," she said. "I want to hear them! Yamil! Miracle! Say something."

Baby's breathing picked up and she started gasping for breath. Charlie grabbed her arm to help calm her.

Sky took Baby's weapon from her while she doubled over in place, clutching her chest. Charlie shook his head, for he knew Sky was about to act brashly.

"Come out," the voice called from the darkness. "Come out and meet your fate. It's the only way you will see those boys again."

"You're a liar!" Sky said.

She stood up and fired through the serving windows, spraying the room beyond with bullets hoping to hit something. All she did was inspire an insidious laughter.

"You know," the voice said, undisturbed by the gunfire, "this place has seen a lot of death and sacrifice. The grounds around us are filled with ashes and dust. It's the perfect place to die."

"I'll remember you said that," Sky said.

Baby's breaths became shallower.

All Sky wanted was Yamil and Miracle. She wanted to see them. She wanted to hold them. She wanted to hear them.

"It's time," the man said. "Come get your boys. See for yourself if they are dead or alive."

Sky agreed. She jumped up and ran for the door leading to the other side. Once there, she opened fire until the clip ran out of ammunition. She then tossed the gun aside and listened for movement. She heard nothing. Nervously, she pulled out her flashlight and shone it around the former dining hall. She saw nothing.

"Come out, you coward, and bring me my boys!" she screamed.

"Sky, wait!" Charlie implored. "He's trying to goad you to expose yourself."

Sky looked back at him but could only see his and Baby's shadow. She ran back to Baby's side, and she was breathing more evenly and seeming more composed.

"Are you okay?" Sky asked.

"Getting there," she huffed. "What happened to the man?"

"I don't know," she said. "I'm going to keep going through the house. You stay here and wait for me."

"I'm going back out the way we came and coming in through the front," Charlie said. "To make sure he doesn't run. I don't get the sense there is anyone else here except the one man. We got this."

"I can't just sit here while you guys—"

"We'll be fine," Charlie said.

Sky handed the M-16 back to Baby. "Reload it and be ready."

Baby nodded. "I'm sorry."

"Don't be," Sky said. "We're going to get out of here soon. With Yamil and Miracle."

Baby regarded Sky with sympathy, as if she didn't believe those words. At least not all of them. Sky noticed her doubt, but chose to ignore it and keep the faith that the boys were there and waiting for her somewhere in the dark corners of the home.

Sky went through the dining hall while Charlie went back through the kitchen to exit from where they had entered. Baby remained, taking in deep breaths.

Twenty-Five

AMON RETRIEVED A CANDLE from the living room mantle, as well as a kerosene lantern. Vash held Misty and Leo at gunpoint and instructed them to lead the way out the door through the kitchen.

Dusk gave way to darkness, but it was a cloudy night, and the moon was tucked deep behind them, offering only a muted light over the property.

"What are you doing?" Misty asked. "This is crazy."

"Your opinion means little to us," Vash said. "Our purpose has been fulfilled. We have control over the fortress and grounds, and our resurrection ceremony shall begin."

"There's nobody in the fortress, Vash," Amon reminded. "Should any of their friends return, there will be no guarantees we can hold it."

"This won't take long," Vash said. "Once we are done here, we shall return inside and prepare our fortification. Seems their friends are all indisposed at the moment."

He turned to Leo and Misty, who were powerless to intervene as their hands were still bound.

"Tell me where the body pit is where you cremated Zagan," Vash demanded.

"Do you really think you are going to return Zagan from the dead?" Misty asked.

"Where is it?" he insisted, ignoring her inquisition.

Misty, hoping to delay the proceedings to buy the unoccupied fortress more time, lied to him. "It's to the left of the compound behind the cemetery."

"Very well, then," he said. "Lead the way."

As he continued pointing the gun at their backs, Misty slowly marched to the back corner of the lot behind Usland and stopped at a wall of shrubbery that lined their compound and the side street that bordered it.

"I guess it's on the other side," Misty said.

Vash withdrew his sword from its sheath and held it to Misty's neck. "You're delaying the inevitable, child, and testing my patience."

Misty could only assume the sword at her neck was the one that had killed JZ, and she grew furious, yet there was little she could do at the moment.

She walked them to the other side of the property beyond Restland, where there was a large shallow hole used to burn bodies collected en masse. They had only two burnings since the fortress was conceived. One was after the probing attack when Zagan first revealed himself, and the other after the full-on assault of the fortress. Zagan's corpse was the last body they threw on top of the pile, which included dozens of the marauders that had laid siege upon the fortress. The smoke from the fire had risen in thick black plumes, which blocked out part of the sky.

"Collect the wood," he commanded Amon.

Amon went about collecting wood from the edge of the forest and built a tent with it at the foot of the pit. Vash dumped kerosene on top of the wooden tent and lit it with the flame of the lantern.

He took one of the extra sticks and walked into the center of the pit. Amon guarded Misty and Leo, who stood in awe as Vash drew a large pentagram in the middle of the body pit. The pentagram was cast alight by the roaring fire. As Vash walked back, his eyes reflected the orange and red of the flames, which made him look possessed.

He lit the candle with the lantern light and placed it to the side of the pit.

"It's time," he said.

"Sit down," Amon commanded the children, who sat crisscross on the edge of the pit.

Amon stood on one side of the fire as Vash stood on the other. They raised their arms and began to chant.

For thou, who perished in the flame, heed this call, rise, and reclaim. Trek on through the mortal door, assemble flesh and walk once more. Zagan, hear us, follow our voice, return to this world, and let Satan rejoice!

The men continued to chant the same line repeatedly as the fire raged. Each time they said it, their voices grew in intensity.

Misty and Leo looked around as small droplets of rain started to dot their skin. As the men continued their chant a large wind kicked up and the flame of the candle on the side of the pit blew out.

Vash saw this and screamed out in joy. "He is here! Arise from the pit, Zagan! Arise! *Ave Satanas*!"

Leo and Misty, growing cold and curious, searched the area with Vash and Amon, wondering with wild anticipation if Zagan might walk out of the woods, human and complete.

"I feel you, Zagan! Assemble your flesh! Assemble your flesh!"

Amid Vash's pronouncements, Misty did see something odd. It was multiple moving lights emanating from the area around the fortress. She swallowed hard as the lights intertwined and raced in many different directions.

"It's him," Vash said, seeing the same lights. He pointed with elation. "His spirit is assembling. He will walk again!"

As the lights got closer, it was Leo who noticed the truth. "He *is* here. King is here."

The rain picked up and the wind swept in once again and stirred the larger fire. King, Wyatt, Teddy, Malayah, and Frankie, followed by the multitude of other civilians who came from the heights to lend support, filled the backyard around the area of the fire and the pit.

When they got close enough, Vash and Amon deflated. The gang of people stopped only feet away.

As King shone his light upon Leo and Misty, Teddy ran over to them and hugged them. Other members of the party turned to the pit and saw the pentagram that was scratched into the earth.

Vash, shocked but not disgraced, cried out. "I know you're here, Zagan! The wind came. The candle blew out. Reveal yourself!"

King raised his handgun and fired off one shot, which struck Vash's neck. Vash clutched his throat as he choked on blood. He dropped to his knees. King walked up to him, reminded of the image of JZ hanging lifeless on the tree; reminded of what Zagan did to Sim and the others.

"You know what the last thing was that Zagan saw in this life?" King asked as Vash choked on blood. King raised his gun. "It was my face, and this gun. You'll always share that in common. And I promise you, nobody's ever going to try to bring you back."

He shot Vash in the head, and he fell to the ground, lifeless.

Amon took off running, but Malayah and Frankie chased after him.

"Not so fast, *puta*!" Frankie yelled.

Shortly thereafter, Amon's screams were heard in the night sky.

The rainfall gained momentum, and the fire began to die. Teddy used a pocketknife to cut Misty and Leo's bindings. Leo ran to the pit and trampled out the pentagram.

"Charlie told us about what happened," Misty said. "I'm glad you're okay, but I knew you would outsmart them."

"We heard about Yamil and Miracle from Wyatt," King said. "Any word?"

"They left a while ago to chase after these two because they thought they would be running back to where Yamil and Miracle were being held in order to harm them. But these guys stayed to fulfill some screwy ritual that they were convinced would bring Zagan back from the dead."

King shook his head.

"You know it's probably a good thing that these guys stayed, because whoever has Yamil and Miracle has no idea what's coming," Wyatt said.

Malayah and Frankie returned from out of the darkness. Malayah was wiping a large hunting knife streaked with blood across her pant leg.

"It's been a hell of a day," Frankie said. "So, this is the fortress?" She looked upon it with wonder.

Malayah put her arm around Frankie, and the two took in the sight of the large building, which was a castle-like shadow in the muted moonlight.

"Should we go after them?" Leo asked, rubbing his wrists to alleviate the cuts caused by the zip ties.

"I think it would be pointless," Misty said. "We'll wait a day before we decide upon another course of action. And in the meantime, we can pray for their safe return."

With the rain now pouring, King yelled, "You are all invited into the fortress for the night. Though it's too early to celebrate a full victory, we can at least be warm and be thankful we all made it through the day."

"Um," Leo said. "It's kind of a bloodbath in there, and there are a few dead bodies to step over on the porch."

"As long as it isn't *our* dead bodies, who cares," King said.

With that, about twenty-five people filed into the fortress. Some gathered around the fireplace while others conversed in the dining room. Some helped Misty clean the floors and walls, and others helped move bodies in the rain to the body pit. The only body they kept at the foot of Usland was Skinny Jim.

He would be buried the next day in full honor alongside JZ.

Twenty-Six

Sky and Charlie diverged, leaving Baby in the kitchen to recover from her panic attack as they pursued the boys in the home.

Sky recovered her flashlight and withdrew a pistol from her bag, creeping quietly into the former dining room. She flashed her light around and cringed. There were some mattresses on the ground, but the windows were boarded up, and floor and walls were peeling paint. As she shuffled across the floor, she heard the crunching of broken glass.

She wondered how anyone could reside in such a place.

There was no sign of anyone. She listened for sounds above or below but heard nothing. She left the dining area, gun raised, through a doorway that led to a blue and red square-tiled foyer. Off this foyer was the front entrance of the building on her right and in front of a former reception area that had a single white rocking chair between it and the door. On her left was a bathroom, the right side of the wall of which had been somehow obliterated, revealing jagged edges of concrete.

There was a set of stairs across from the bathroom leading to the second floor. She arched her neck to get a look, but it was too dark. She listened for sound but still heard nothing.

The main entrance door squeaked open, and Sky spun around, preparing to fire, but it was only Charlie. He entered on tiptoes and closed the wooden door behind him.

"That was quick," Sky whispered.

"Nothing out there," he said. "This guy has to be a lone wolf, but where did he go?"

"I don't know," she said. "Let's clear the first floor and then move to the second."

She proceeded away from the main entrance and down the hallway running between the stairs and bathroom. The hallway wrapped around to the back portion of the house where there were a series of rooms. She popped her head into each one, believing that at any moment someone was going to jump out of a dark corner and attack her. Charlie walked with his back to hers, keeping an eye out behind them.

One of the rooms she looked into had a lantern burning in the far corner, the light from which revealed two mattresses set up in perpendicular fashion, but a distance away from each other. Her light revealed three windows in the bedroom, two of which had boards covering them, but the third was intact and the window ajar.

Sky doubled checked the mattresses and shined the light back at the open window. She entered the room and Charlie waited at the door, his own flashlight directed toward the areas outside the room.

Sky leaned down and shook the blankets on each mattress, as if Yamil and Miracle might magically appear from underneath. They didn't, of course, but what she found curious was her discovery of several pieces of rope and what looked to be a sash of some sort.

She shined her light on it. The rope was frayed at the ends. She picked it up and examined it more closely. It looked like a piece of rope that had been cut. As she continued to shine her light around the room, she found three other pieces of rope with the same frayed edges. The other three were near the second mattress. After reviewing the pieces of rope, she flashed her light back to the window. She returned to Charlie's side.

"I know it's hard to believe," Sky said, holding the rope up. "But I think they could have escaped." She shined the light on the mattresses and windows. "It looks like they might have been held here, and somehow cut the ropes and got out the window."

Charlie shined his own flashlight in on the mattresses and window. He regarded the ropes that Sky held with curiosity.

"I suppose anything is possible," he said. "They are little, but they had the same training as you all did. If they knew they were in danger, they might have acted."

"We can't take that for granted, though," Sky said. "Maybe that guy cut them loose and took them with him when he knew we were here. We have to check the second floor."

Initially, Sky harbored a level of satisfaction and contentment when she thought the boys might have escaped, but then her mind wandered.

Are they really any better off out there on their own?

"Let's get back to the stairway," Sky said.

Charlie led the way back around the corner and down the corridor to the foyer and stairway.

"Are we wasting our time?" Sky asked. "He could be up there waiting to ambush us, and the kids may not even be there. I don't hear any noise at all."

As she weighed her options, a voice from the second floor whispered.

"Come see your boys," he called. "Free them."

She moved around to the foot of the stairs.

"If they are with you, let me hear one of them speak and I will come for them," she said.

"The cat has their tongues," the man said. "And soon will have the rest of them."

"You're lying!" Sky said. "They escaped, didn't they? Let me hear them. Now!"

The man did not return a comment.

"Your useless plan has been foiled," Charlie yelled up. "I killed one of your men, and the other two ran off like cowards. We discovered your little plan with the heights militia and killed them all. The fortress is ours, and you are the last one. It's over."

"Not while you still seek your little friends," the man said.

Sky, confident that the boys were not on the second floor, reached into her bag. She withdrew Kellogg's coin and rubbed it between her thumb and forefinger. She put it back into the bag and exchanged it for a grenade. She pulled the pin and slowly walked up the stairs. It wound around to the second floor.

"What are you doing?" Charlie asked.

"Ending this," Sky said.

She listened closely as she ascended, stopping short about three steps from the top. She arched her neck around and to the right noticed a large open area that resembled a living room. Straight ahead was another corridor.

"I'm here," she said.

She then rolled the grenade down the corridor and fled back down the stairwell. She and Charlie ran into the dining hall. Seconds later, an explosion erupted, and the screams of a single man were heard. The ceiling shook, and dust and debris rained down onto the first floor.

When the dust settled, the two sighed in relief.

"I'll go up to make sure it's clear," Charlie said. "You make sure Baby is okay."

Sky ran back through the dining room and into the kitchen as Charlie made a move back to the stairs.

"Holy cow," Baby said when Sky entered. "What happened?"

"He was on the second floor," Sky said as she pulled Baby forward. "I tossed a grenade."

"You didn't find them?" Baby asked.

"Charlie is double-checking," Sky said. "But I don't think they're here. I think they might have escaped."

"Escaped?" Baby said. "Yamil and Miracle?"

"I think I saw where they were kept," Sky said. "There were mattresses, an open window, and ropes that had been cut."

"Could they have?" Baby pondered.

"I don't know," Sky said. "I just know what I saw, and if they aren't here then—"

Charlie entered the kitchen breathing heavily. "All clear up there. The boys aren't there and that guy...Let's just say his membership in their Satanic cult just lapsed."

"Okay, then," Sky said. "If they made it out of the place through that open window, it would have led them out back. Let's go."

The rain was coming down hard at that point. They snatched ponchos from their side bags and draped themselves before leaving. They circled around to the rear of the property to the open window and traced a line from the window to the woods with their flashlights.

"Do you think they went that way?" Charlie asked.

"Who knows," Sky said. "If they got this far, they probably would have just run into the woods, right? It's only natural."

"Wouldn't we have run into them on our way here if they managed to escape somehow?" Baby asked.

"I don't know," Sky said, her voice stifled by the sound of the falling rain. "I'm doing the best I can here."

"Let's just check the woods and see where it leads us," Charlie said.

Sky thought of the boys in the rain. They didn't have protective gear or a flashlight. How would they even manage?

They entered the forest beyond the yard. Sky kept point with Baby and Charlie behind her. They called out Yamil and Miracle's names repeatedly as they made it through to the other side and onto a dirt road, which crossed over to another set of trees and followed the road down.

"Woods or road?" Baby asked.

It was anyone's guess where the boys would have gone if they made it to the same crossroads. Sim had always told them to keep a low profile outside, so if the boys had followed that protocol, they would have stayed in the trees but followed the path of the road.

The three stayed on the road and followed it all the way down. It led them to the main road, about fifty yards north of Redemption Road. Sky turned her head in both directions. It was hard to see through the heavy rain.

"There is only one of two ways they could have gone," Sky said.

"Hopefully they chose the road back toward home," Baby said.

"If we go right, we'll probably walk miles the wrong way for nothing in this rain," Charlie said. "If they escaped that place, at this point, we can only hope they find their way back, Sky. We can't keep up this search any longer. We need to go back for now."

Reluctantly, Sky agreed. It was hopeless to know which way the boys had gone, or if they had even escaped at all. They could be dead and buried. Sky shook away the thought, as she didn't want to cry. She was miserable enough.

They headed back down the long road to the fortress. Had it not been pitch dark and pouring rain, they might have noticed the small house with the fenced in front yard that was set back from the highway, which they passed not too long after returning to the main road.

As it were, they traveled through the night and the downpour all the way back to the fortress. They arrived just before dawn, after the rain had finally subsided. They were exhausted and weary. To their surprise, however, they were met with the warm embraces of King and all the others, including men and women from the heights who had come to their rescue.

It was comforting and surprising to hear all of the new details of the drama that had unfolded while they were on the road. The others were sad, of course, that Yamil, Miracle, and Gigi had not been found, but relieved that the last of the opposing men had been handled.

There would be peace again. And though it was hard to stomach, that peace would come with or without Yamil and Miracle.

Twenty-Seven

THE NEXT MORNING, THERE was a glorious breakfast at the fortress, with lots of eggs, juice, fruit, and johnny cakes. It was enjoyed by all.

Laughter, chatter, and comradery filled every room of the large home. Those who had never been to the fortress enjoyed tours and views of the city skyline from the rooftop. Charlie was overwhelmed with appreciation and humbled by the heights' response to Tony's siege.

If this isn't the biggest testimony to the strength of our established order, I don't know what is.

After clean-up, they buried Skinny Jim in Usland with a formal ceremony, so it was convenient to have a multitude of heights community members on hand to help remember him.

Sky was the last one to comment, placing a flower on top of the fresh grave.

"I'm sorry, Jim," Sky said. "I doubted you in the beginning, and I feel ashamed. I hope you have found peace with your mother, father, sister, and aunt. I hope they know what a gift you were to this world, and I hope you will continue to watch over us all."

Around noon, many of the heights members left the fortress for home. Charlie, Malayah, and Frankie remained to attend a committee meeting with Wyatt and the others, which was held in the dining room on this occasion.

The meeting began with a discussion of another search party for the boys.

"I would like to lead the next search party," King said. "This time, going up, we'll take the highway route in case they came back that way. If we don't have any luck crossing paths, we'll pass beyond Redemption Road and go as far south as we feel is necessary before calling it quits. We'll leave as soon as this meeting adjourns."

"I'll go with you, King," Malayah said. "Frankie, too."

"You're darn straight," she said. "We'll find them."

"I will send Jack and his crew down to replace the windows and other damage in the house once I get back," Charlie said.

"Make sure you give props to Mrs. Chandler, man," King said. "She surely saved the day yesterday. It's people like her that you wouldn't even think would rise to the occasion that are the most valuable to our communities."

"Oh, I always knew there was something special about that girl aside from her dental qualifications," Wyatt said.

"She is a sweet lady, for sure," Charlie said. "And I will certainly extend my appreciation for her intervention. On a similar note, Malayah and Frankie, as soon you return to the heights, I would like to put you in charge of our community militia. I think you're perfect to replace Tony and inspire continued trust in our defense team."

"We got you, Charlie," Frankie said. "And I won't even say we told you so about that *puta*, Tony."

"But, you just did," Charlie said.

"Oh, damn. Sorry, Charlie," she said.

"All in all, we overcame," Charlie said. "God rest JZ's soul with prayers that Yamil and Miracle are alive and come back home. This has only made us stronger."

Sky became teary-eyed at that and adjourned the meeting. As everyone pushed out their chairs, Misty radioed from the roof.

"Oh my God, guys," she said, her voice wavering. "I'm coming down. You have to see this. Go out front."

After their visit to the hair and nail salon, the trio, along with Gigi, made no additional stops. They walked the long road to the highway, and then took the highway all the way to the green bridge. When Yamil and Miracle saw the bridge, they took deep breaths and smiled larger than they ever had before.

Yamil jumped up and down and hugged Miracle. Harlow smiled, but admitted she was going to miss them.

She led them over the green bridge, and as they approached the intersection, she stopped them alongside a curb and next to a storm drain. She slid the iron cover aside while the boys and Gigi watched with curious attention.

"What are you doing?" Miracle asked.

"This is where I get off, kids," Harlow said.

Yamil and Miracle peered down into the hole. There was a rusty ladder that led down into the dark void.

"Down there?" Yamil said.

"I told you it could wait for another day." She smiled.

Harlow gave each one a hug, then stepped into the hole and onto the ladder. When she was halfway down the shaft, she looked up to them.

"I'll see you again...soon," she said. "You can meet my friends."

Gigi licked her face and whined as Miracle and Yamil waved goodbye. Then Harlow pulled the cover back over the hole. And just like that, she was gone.

Miracle and Yamil took each other's hands and walked to the intersection with Gigi at their side. They paused at the bottom of the hill and took in the sight of the mighty fortress. Their home. Seeing it again was like a dream.

As they started their final journey from the intersection to the fortress, the blue doors sprung open, and Sky, followed by all the other orphans, ran out into the street.

Yamil and Miracle smiled and broke into a sprint.

Sky, overcome with tears, ran as fast as she could down the hill as the others chased behind. When they met, she scooped them both up, one in each arm, and tears of joy flowed. Sky fell to her knees as the boys each placed a head on one of her shoulders. She held them like that until all the others arrived while Gigi wagged her tail and licked them all.

Back at the fortress, Wyatt, Charlie, Malayah, and Frankie stood at the top of the steps, relishing the moment.

"I guess we can call off that search party," Malayah said.

All the other orphans formed a circle around the boys. They took turns leaning down and hugging them as Yamil unloaded the pack from his back. He unzipped it and pulled out the picture of JZ that he had gotten from the hair and nail salon.

Everyone took turns passing it around and looking at it. Of course, they all wanted to know the story of how he got it, and their bigger adventure beyond that. For the moment, though, they all huddled together, crying and laughing in the middle of the street holding JZ's picture.

Sky, King, Misty, Baby, Teddy, Leo, Yamil, Miracle, and Gigi.

The fortress.

Twenty-Eight

At breakfast the next morning, the others were already eating when Teddy came down later than usual, sulking.

"What's the matter?" Sky said. "You're not your usual Teddy self."

"My tooth necklace is missing. The one that King made for me. I know I took it off from around my neck last night. I put it right on the nightstand." Teddy looked at Leo. "You remember me taking it off, don't you, Leo?"

Leo shrugged. "I remember you having nightmares again, but that's about it."

"It was there," Teddy cried. "And it disappeared."

"Call up to King on the roof," Wyatt suggested. "I have a feeling he may be able to point you in the right direction."

Sky handed Teddy a walkie talkie.

"King," Teddy said. "King, do you hear me?"

"What's up?" he said. "Is that you, Baby?"

Teddy cringed. "What do you mean, 'baby'?"

Everyone around the table laughed.

"Just kidding, Teddy,' King said. "Shouldn't you have a mouthful of oatmeal by now?"

"Wyatt said you might know where my tooth necklace went," Teddy said.

"I don't exactly know where it is, Teddy," King said. "But I do remember the Tooth Fairy takes lost teeth in the middle of the night. I also remember that she always gives you something in return."

Teddy thought back to those days, and how he used to find dollar bills under his pillow after placing a tooth under it before he went to bed. His face suddenly lit up. He gave back the walkie talkie to Sky and ran like the wind up the two flights of stairs to his room on the third floor. He went to his bed and lifted his pillow. Underneath was another necklace. This one was made with a brown shoelace and a small wooden chess piece.

Teddy smiled and put the necklace around his neck. He ran back downstairs, proudly displaying it.

"Very nice, Teddy," Wyatt said. "Fashionable."

He took back the walkie talkie from Sky and radioed up to King.

"The Tooth Fairy left me another necklace," Teddy said.

King then said, "I saw it. I hope it will always remind you that, although I am the King, you will always be my number one knight."

"It will." Teddy smiled, remembering how King saved his life. "It will."

Dear Diary,

There is so much to say. We defeated another foe, without Sim, but with him. That was the irony of everything. These men, they wanted to bring Zagan back from the dead, and the only thing they accomplished was making Sim a revenant for the fortress. For in our dire need, Sim returned, and reminded us of all the things he taught us and the reasons why we should always fight for the new world. Love, the double-edged sword, I learned is actually only a sword that cuts one way, because even in our weakest moments, love prevails.

Tomorrow, dear Sim, we shall bury your journals alongside you, for everything we need to know about you is already known, and the rest...is yours to hold. Maybe JZ was right about that.

Speaking of tomorrow, we wonder what it will bring. I still yearn for my uncle and wonder of his fate. I wonder about the fortress and the heights and the next threat, should it arise. It's exciting to anticipate all the glorious things that may be revealed in time but are yet unknown. It gives me hope and promise.

What will always be the same, though, is my love for the fortress and my brothers and sisters, past and present, who will be my rock for everything I do. Every decision I make.

We are the fortress, and the fortress is us.

Thank you, Sim.

Sky closed her journal and put her back on her pillow as she remembered the last supper they had with Sim.

The dining room at the fortress was always crowded. Sim had them move in two more tables so that everyone could always fit, so the dining room extended into another sitting room that was in the front of the house.

Sim tapped his glass with a fork to get everyone's attention.

"Good evening, my children," he said. "Back in regular times, when someone tapped a glass with a fork at a wedding like I just did, it would mean there was about to be a toast."

"I like toast," Yamil said.

"Not toast, Yamil," Sim said. "A toast. A speech."

"Okay," Shark said. "Let's hear it, Sim. We all love your speeches."

Several of the children laughed.

"With Yamil and Miracle leaving for the heights tomorrow, and with Zagan's pending siege, this may be the last time we are all together as a family. Of course, King is not with us, but I hope one day you can share with him this moment. You can tell him, I love him. I love all of you. You gave me purpose when there was none. You gave me life, when there was nothing but death. You gave the new world hope. We don't have to worry about winning against Zagan or any other foe that should follow, because we have already won. Remember that. I told my first orphan, Elizabeth, to prepare her heart as a fortress, for there will be no other. And I tell you the same. Bless this day, and all others that follow. Be still, for God is with us."

Everyone raised their glasses following Sim's lead, and they tapped the edges of those glasses together. There was the sound of dinging throughout the extended living room.

"Now, children," Sim said. "I would like to go around the table as if it were a Thanksgiving meal, which it kind of is, because we have a turkey, and have each of you tell us what you are thankful for. Let's start with Ace."

"Whoa," Ace said. "Let me think. Well, I'm thankful for my family. My brother, sister, parents...and all of you. What more can I say? Family has been everything for me. And how lucky was I to see the end of the world, and still have a family. So...I guess, family."

JZ, realizing she was next, rubbed her arms with a bit of discomfort. "I know this sounds weird, but the Lord does tell us to pray and ask for forgiveness. And Zagan did bring us together and taught us the value of our love."

"So, you are thankful for Zagan?" Misty asked, confused.

"No, no," JZ said. "Not like that. Thankful for what he taught us, about each other."

Proceeding down the table, Baby said, "The fortress."

Teddy said, "Flip. He's gone, but he was my best friend. We had a secret handshake. I really miss him."

Kellogg said, "That I was able to live again, so I could meet all of you. And holding hands with Sky when we explored the tunnel."

"I didn't hold your hand!" Sky said, giggling.

Kellogg laughed. "It was just wishful thinking. Can you blame a guy?"

Yamil said, "Pancakes!" as he raised a fork. Everyone laughed.

Miracle followed suit. "Pancakes!"

Misty said, "Maybe...I guess...yeah, I guess the fortress. What else is there?"

Leo said, "Charlie and the heights. He hasn't gotten a shoutout, and he deserves one."

Shark said, "My mom and dad. They taught me what's right."

Big Will said, "Gigi, and all of you." He reached down and pet Gigi on the top of her head.

Finally, Sky said, "Well, all of you of course, but my Uncle Mike, because he kept me safe and led me here. If it weren't for him, I would never have found you."

"Okay, then," Sim said. "Thanks for sharing, my children. Let's eat and be happy. For reality is right now, not tomorrow and not yesterday."

And so they ate, and enjoyed the moment. Because at any moment that's all that life is: short moments savored for long years.

Epilogue

Two months after the fall of Vash, King alerted the others by walkie talkie that a group of six men on horseback was approaching the fortress. Sky immediately worried that it could spell another threat for the community.

As she made her way to the front with Wyatt and Misty, she thought of her Uncle Mike.

"What is going on around here lately?" Sky asked over her walkie talkie.

Two weeks prior, the bridges leading in and out of a small island just outside of the city had been detonated. The explosions upon the bridges were observed from the rooftop of the fortress and heard as far away as the heights.

She flung open the doors to the fortress, and she, along with Wyatt and Misty, thrust semi-automatic weapons in the horsemen's direction.

They had changed their vetting process after what happened with Ms. Betty. No longer was anyone allowed to stay at the fortress for any amount of time, and they were more closely scrutinizing people to send to the heights.

Live and learn.

"What do you people—"

Sky stopped mid-sentence and dropped her gun to the ground. Her body fell backward into the foyer.

Wyatt and Misty looked at her, fainted on the floor, then back at the horseman.

"Sorry about that," a bearded man decked in flannel said from atop one of the horses. "I had a feeling she might react that way."

"Why?" Misty asked. "Who are *you*?"

He smiled broadly. "I'm her Uncle Mike."

THE END OF REVANENT.

Find out what happens to the orphans next in Book 3, KINGDOM.

About the Author

T.A. Styles earned his B.S. in Elementary Education and Mathematics and his M.S. in Developmental Reading. He taught in elementary and junior high schools for twelve years before launching his own childcare enterprise, TSL Kids Crew, which he has operated since 2009. He has had a passion for writing stories since he was a teenager, as it was a hobby and skill for which he realized at a young age he had a knack for and loved. He has two grown children and has traveled extensively including to Iceland, Australia, Greece, Italy, South America, and many other places nationally and internationally.

Connect with him at www.tastyles.com.